THE PAYOFF

LYNNE CANTWELL

hearth/myth

Table of Contents

Also by Lynne Cantwell:

The Elemental Keys
River Magic
Bog Magic
Gecko Magic
Beach Magic

The Pipe Woman Chronicles Universe
Seized: Book One of the Pipe Woman Chronicles
Fissured: Book Two of the Pipe Woman Chronicles
Tapped: Book Three of the Pipe Woman Chronicles
Gravid: Book Four of the Pipe Woman Chronicles
Annealed: Book Five of the Pipe Woman Chronicles
The Pipe Woman Chronicles Omnibus

Where Were You When: A Land, Sea, Sky Anthology
Crosswind: Land, Sea, Sky Book 1
Undertow: Land, Sea, Sky Book 2
Scorched Earth: Land, Sea, Sky Book 3
The Land Sea Sky Trilogy

Dragon's Web: Book One of the Pipe Woman's Legacy
Firebird's Snare: Book Two of the Pipe Woman's Legacy
Spider's Lifeline: Book Three of the Pipe Woman's Legacy
Turtle's Weir: Book Four of the Pipe Woman's Legacy

A Billion Gods and Goddesses: The Mythology Behind *The Pipe Woman Chronicles*

Interested in a free novel?

Join my mailing list at http://eepurl.com/wwx9d!

Life, if well lived, is long enough.

— Seneca

New Mexico

Chapter 1 — Late May

Mrs. Janis Fowler, librarian at El Camino Real High School, raised her gaze to the young man standing before her. She shot him a dubious look over the top of her reading glasses. "Mr. Goodson," she said, "there is no such thing as Good and Evil."

The young man feigned shock. "Mrs. Fowler! That's blasphemy!"

"Not in my religion," she went on relentlessly. "In my religion, we don't shift blame for our actions to outmoded concepts of morality."

"Oh?" the boy said with a sneer. "So what do you blame instead?"

"Our choices," she said. "Which have consequences." She dropped her eyes to the ripped, burned carcass of *To Kill a Mockingbird* lying on the desk before her. "You *will* be charged for what you have done to this book, Mr. Goodson. And if you don't settle that debt, you won't graduate with your class next month."

Chad Goodson fumed for a moment. Then a veil seemed to fall over his features. "Expect a call from my father, Mrs. Fowler."

She felt the graying bun atop her head jiggle as she laughed. Out of the corner of her eye, she saw her student assistant turn in her seat, take in the scene, and smirk. "Your father may scare *you*, but he doesn't scare *me*," Mrs. Fowler assured him, even as images tumbled before her mind's eye: Chad's father with his hand raised to both the boy and his mother; a belt wielded on the backside of a much younger version of the father by a wickedly gleeful woman; that woman as a child, knocked across the room by her own father; and on and on, backward in time, a family tree of pain and fear. And they had the temerity to call it love.

She almost felt sorry for the young man who stood before her. She knew what his bravado hid; she had seen it many times before in her forty years at this school. But then her eyes dropped to the ruined book on the desk, and she knew she could make it stop. Moreover, she *needed* to make it stop. Chad's parents had younger children, too.

"Please do have him call me," she told the boy. "I'd like to talk to him."

Surprised, he stepped back. Then his eyes narrowed. "I think you're lying," he said. "I don't think you believe in anything. I think you're a Godless heathen."

A bell rang. Mrs. Fowler smiled pleasantly. "Don't be late for class, Mr. Goodson. Your father won't be pleased if you end up in detention."

Furious, he spun on his heel and marched to the door. "Creepy old hag," he muttered, just loud enough for her to hear.

"Have a nice day," she called after him as he slammed open one of the double doors into the hallway. Someone caught it on the rebound.

As the man's face came into view, Mrs. Fowler gasped. It had been more than forty years since she had last seen him and time had taken its toll, as it had on her. But there could be no mistake – it was in the set of his shoulders, his presence in the doorway, the mixed emotions apparent on his face: hope and pain, satisfaction and fear.

She was sure her expression mirrored his.

"Teresa," she said, turning to the student assistant. "Would you please make sure Chad's account is charged for the book?"

"Wow. He really did a number on it," she said, frowning. "He's such a jerk. Doesn't he have any respect for anything?"

Mrs. Fowler could have given quite a detailed answer. Instead, she rose. "I'll be in my office," she said, self-consciously perching her readers on top of her hair.

Teresa looked from her to the man still standing in the doorway. Kids were ducking into the room under his outstretched arm. "Who is that guy? I've never seen him before. Is he a sub?"

"No," Mrs. Fowler said shortly. "He has no connection to this school." She stepped away from the circulation desk and motioned the man toward the door to her office.

4

He started, as if her gesture had brought him back from a million miles away. Handing off the door to a young man not much taller than he was, he followed Mrs. Fowler into the tiny room. She was suddenly aware of how cramped it was – between the desk, the chairs, and the bookshelves, there was hardly room to turn around – and how vulnerable she felt. How exposed. How young, and yet how very, very old.

He shut the door and took her into his arms. "Janis," he breathed.

"Jan," she said, and began to cry. She had not said his name in decades – had not trusted herself to utter it aloud, lest it call him to her. Now it was all right, he was already here, so she could say it – and in the proper way, with the J sounding like a Y, not like Dr. Tandy...

She shuddered. She had not allowed herself to think of that awful woman for decades, either.

"Shhh," Jan murmured into her hair. He lifted her readers from her head and gently unwound the cord that held them around her neck. She let go of him long enough to take the glasses from him, fold them properly, and place them on her desk. Then she looked up at him.

Janusz Marek was just as tall as he had been when they had parted. Age had not bent him, although his hairline had receded and the long, lush brown hair she remembered had gone salt-and-pepper with a corporate-job cut. He was still thin, but not painfully so, his wrists still bony and his fingers still long. His eyes, too, were the same – a clear blue so arresting that she hardly noticed the crow's feet. He wore khakis and a blue dress shirt, as if he had just stopped by on his way home from work.

She knew time had taken a wrecking ball to her looks. Her hair, once long, straight, and blond, was now more white than gray; she piled it atop her head to camouflage the spots where her scalp showed through. She had been thin, too, once – willowy, even – but she had developed a comfortable layer of padding over the years, thanks to her sedentary job and her tendency to spend her free time alone.

He could not possibly see her as he once had. They had grown up together, two halves of one, meeting in the middle between her ability to see the past and his to read the future. Dr. Tandy and the others at the Institute had enabled it. Encouraged it. *Demanded* it.

Which is why it had to stop. Why they had to be the ones to stop it.

It had been so hard to leave him. Necessary, but *so hard*.

And now here he was, and she knew what that meant: the life she had put on hold so long ago was about to resume. The stakes would be high. But Jan would be by her side again.

That almost made it worth the wait. That, and the certainty that all the choices Dr. Tandy had made were about to reap the consequences she so richly deserved.

Chapter 2 — Two weeks earlier

Jan Marek looked up from the spreadsheet on his computer and grinned at the guy standing in his office doorway. "What's going on, Ed?"

The younger man leaned a shoulder against the door jamb, arms and ankles crossed. "I didn't mean to interrupt, Jan." He pronounced it like the girl's name – like the middle sister on *The Brady Bunch* – just as everyone at the office did. Jan never bothered to correct them. "I just stopped by to let you know that some of the guys are going out for a beer after work. Want to join us?"

"Can't," Jan said, gesturing at his computer. "Gotta finish this for the boss."

"Of course. I don't know why I even bother to ask anymore."

Jan shrugged. "What can I say? You know I'm not much for socializing."

Ed rolled his eyes in exasperation. "This isn't a *party*, for God's sake. It's just a few guys getting together for a beer. Blowing off some steam at the end of the week. You know."

"Yeah, I know. Blowing off steam and cruising for chicks, or whatever you young studs call it these days."

Ed's laugh was loud and hearty. "Okay, Boomer," he said cheerfully.

"Bah," said Jan, waving him off with a grin.

Ed eyed him speculatively. "You know, there's a rumor that you're not into girls."

"That rumor is older than you are." Jan arched an eyebrow. "Why? Are *you* interested?"

Ed planted both feet on the floor in alarm. "Jesus Christ, Jan! No! And if I were, I like to think I'd be a little more subtle about it!"

Jan laughed. "You? Subtle?"

"Well…" Ed shrugged.

"Right. Not so much. So it's settled. You're straight, and I'm going to stay here and finish this report. You guys have a good time." And he turned back to his monitor.

Ed sighed. "I'm going to keep trying, you know. All work and no play makes Jan a dull boy."

"So I've heard. But I like my own company. And I really do need to get back to this."

"See you Monday," said Ed, and walked away.

Jan watched the man's back as he retreated past the first cubicle wall. The images came to him unbidden: Ed would meet the love of his life tonight. Marnie would be tough on him, but he needed that. They would marry in about a year's time, just before he was diagnosed with cancer, which he would beat with her support. After that scare, they would have a long, happy life.

The things Jan learned when his Sight kicked in weren't always this pleasant, and usually not so clear-cut, but given that he had seen just the one timeline, Ed's future appeared to be assured. He vowed to himself to act surprised when Ed broke the news of his and Marnie's engagement in a few months.

He turned back to the spreadsheet. He knew there was a problem with it, but he also knew it would be an easy fix. He just didn't know yet what the problem was, or how he would fix it – only that it was there and he would. Most of the time, his Sight was a giant, unhelpful pain in the ass. At least this time, he knew he'd be home in time to catch up on a couple of episodes of the show he'd been watching on Netflix. He was grateful once again that his Sight didn't extend to TV shows. At least one aspect of his life still had the power to surprise him.

Half an hour later, he had found the problem he knew was there. Fifteen minutes later, he had it analyzed and patched. He attached the report to an email and sent it to his boss, Dan Abioye. Dan had been with the company for twenty years – about half as long as Jan had. In fact, Jan had supervised Dan when he had first come aboard as an intern, and he'd been thrilled when Dan had been promoted past him.

Jan liked being a senior project manager. He had worked hard for his first fifteen years at Jemez Aerospace to be promoted to the position. Not only did it get him out of the cube farm and into an office with an actual window and a view of the Jemez Mountains, but it was a perfect position for a guy with the Sight: he could see the potential of everyone who walked into his department and could encourage them in just the right way to reach that potential.

Plus the position didn't typically present him with problems he couldn't handle. He'd had a bellyful of complicated problems when he was a teen. He was happy to have put all that behind him, as painful as it had been to… No. He was not going to let himself open that door. Not today. He had lost too many weekends of his life to second-guessing, to dreaming of what might have been, and to brooding of justice long denied. Tonight would be Netflix and chill. Alone.

Firmly, he focused his attention on closing all the apps on his computer, shutting each one down methodically in the prescribed way. He was tired of getting nastygrams from IT about inadvertently violating some security protocol no one had told him about.

The last thing he shut down was his email account. As his mouse pointer traveled toward the big red X in the upper right corner of the screen, a new message popped into his inbox.

A single look at the subject line – **PLEASE READ – NEW CLIENT PROTOCOLS** – gave him a premonition of dread. It wasn't the Sight – not yet. But he was sure he wasn't going to like what he saw when he opened it.

He glanced out the window at the fading afternoon light, then at what he could see of the cube farm from his open office door. It was late. The big brass had obviously waited until everyone was gone for the day before sending this email, intending for everyone to see it first thing Monday morning.

He could do that. He could shut down his laptop right now and walk away, and read the message Monday morning, when everybody else did.

And have this sense of dread hanging over him all weekend? Right. So much for Netflix and chill.

He rubbed his face with both hands. Then he clicked on the message. And as he read it, as his eyes hit on the familiar name, his Sight kicked in and his stomach dropped to his feet. Countless timelines cascaded out from this moment, each one branching and tumbling, but all coalescing at the same inevitable conclusion. The world would be lucky to survive.

Unless...

Jan grabbed onto that thought like a lifeline. He took a deep breath and looked out the window again. The sun had gone behind the mountains, leaving the parking lot in shadow. He could barely see the outline of his SUV.

All those years ago, he had known this was coming. Like the problem in that spreadsheet, he knew it was out there – he just hadn't known what form it would take. Now, today, he did. And he knew what that meant. He knew what he had to do next.

He shut down his computer and pushed his chair back from his desk. At the door of his office, he paused with his hand on the light switch, taking a look around at the personal effects he had accumulated over his forty years with the company: framed certificates for training courses he had completed, Lucite tombstones commemorating successful projects, a single ball cap sporting the company's logo. His desk was bare of everything except his company-issued laptop and an organizer for sticky notes, pens, and his business cards. It wasn't much, but it was perfect for a guy who had been hiding in plain sight for four decades.

He switched off the light and headed out through the darkened building to his car. So much for Netflix and chill. He needed to find Janis.

California, 1960-1971

Chapter 3 — A long time ago

"What did you just say to me?"

The tiny girl jumped. It was never good when Mama spoke to her sharply. "Nothing," she said in a voice so small that the traffic passing overhead drowned her out.

Mama crab-walked closer to her over the slanting concrete surface. "Say that again," she said, her face inches from the girl's. "Louder."

Her mother's scent filled her nostrils: stale sweat and booze, together with another, more rank odor that made her want to wrinkle her nose. But she didn't. That was dangerous, too. "I didn't say anything!" she piped.

"Yes, you did." Mama shook her finger in her face. "You said you knew why I had you."

With wide eyes trained on Mama's fingertip, the little girl could only nod.

"Well?" The fingertip shook again.

The words stuck in her throat. She couldn't force them out. Why was Mama making such a big deal about it, anyway? It was just a passing thought – just like all the others that flitted through her mind and found their way out through her mouth. Sometimes the things she said made Mama laugh. Most of the time Mama said she wished the girl would shut up.

Now, as the silence grew, Mama's lips curled in a sly smile. Her finger touched the tiny girl's chin, tipping her face up. "Tell me and I'll give you candy."

This was almost more frightening than the threat of violence. But just then her empty stomach cramped. "Because… because you wanted to make Gigi and Pete mad." *Piss them off* was the phrase she had heard when the scene had formed in her mind, but she knew better than to say that to Mama.

Abruptly, Mama's finger dropped. After another moment, she said, "Why would they be mad?"

Might as well tell it all now. "Because Pete is my daddy."

Mama breathed in sharply. "Close enough," she said at last, and turned away. "Close enough." She threw the girl a look over her shoulder. "How long have you known?"

"Known what?"

Mama rolled her eyes. "Never mind." And they went back to sitting silently under the overpass.

They sat that way for a long, long time. Then the little girl said, "Mama? Can I have my candy now?"

"There's no candy, Janis," Mama said, looking away off in the distance with what Gigi called her thousand-yard stare. "There's never any candy."

The little girl was used to pain. But something about this felt worse – worse than being yelled at. Worse than being slapped or kicked. This felt like her mother had reached through her chest and ripped out her heart.

It was years before the girl had the vocabulary to name that feeling. Just then, in that moment, all she could do was stick out her bottom lip and wrap her own arms around the place in her chest where her heart used to be.

Late that night, Mama dragged the girl out of a fitful sleep and down the slanting concrete to a waiting car. At first Janis fought back, but then she recognized the car. It was Gigi's. Suddenly she wanted a warm bath and a real bed more than anything in the world. She broke free of Mama's grasp and bolted for the back seat.

Mama got in the front. Then, with a curse, she got back out and buckled Janis into the baby seat in back. Once she was settled in front

14

again, Gigi pulled away. Lulled by the car's warmth and the murmured voices of the two people she loved best in the whole, wide world, Janis fell back to sleep.

The next thing she knew, it was morning, and something smelled delicious. She climbed down from the crib in Mama's old room and went to find Gigi. But as she neared the kitchen, her steps slowed. She could hear Gigi and Mama, their voices rising.

"You'd give up your *child?*" Gigi said. "To those *people?*"

"I don't know what else to do with her," Mama said.

"You don't know what else to do with her? Pete and I will take her! We'd do it in a heartbeat. You know that!"

"You think I'm crazy?" Mama cried. "I'm not letting Pete within ten feet of her! Not after what he did to me!"

"He never did *anything* to you," Gigi hissed.

"Yeah, sure, right," Mama said, sounding tired. "I just had tummy troubles. Ate something that didn't agree with me."

Janis could hear footsteps walking away and then back again. "It was that boy you were seeing. That *awful…*"

"No, it *wasn't,*" Mama said. "Look. We've had this conversation a million times and it never gets us anywhere. And who her father is doesn't matter anyway. Not for this."

"But Kelsie," Gigi pleaded. "Giving up your little girl?"

"*You* thought about it," Mama said. "You almost *did* it. I know. I Saw it."

"But I didn't!" Gigi cried. "It was your father's idea. He couldn't cope with what was going on. But I couldn't go through with it."

"Right. You divorced him to save me."

"And it worked, didn't it?" Gigi said.

"Yeah. And then you married *Pete.*"

The room grew quiet. Janis had slid to a seat on the floor just outside the kitchen doorway, her back against the living room wall. She started to get up, but froze at the tone of sadness in her Gigi's voice.

"You *can't*, Kelsie. They'll never let us see her again."

Mama sighed. "It's better this way. I can't raise her on the streets. I won't. And you won't keep Pete away from her." She paused. "She'll have food and clothes at the Institute. She'll get an education. And they're the only ones who can help her with her talent."

"That's not true," Gigi protested. "You did just fine without their help."

"No, I didn't," Mama said. "Don't lie, Mom. And it's only going to get worse. You know it will." Mama walked rapidly out the doorway and past Janis without even seeing her. Janis watched her warily. Then she got up and went into the kitchen.

"There's my little pumpkin pie!" Gigi said, scooping her up for a hug and kiss. "How are you this morning? What would you like for breakfast?"

A few days later, the three of them were back in Gigi's car, driving on unfamiliar streets to a place in the country. Janis marveled at the scenery inside the big gates. Green grass! Tall trees! And a big building with littler ones around it, all spread out with room between them – not like in the city, where the buildings were taller and bunched together, with only concrete separating them.

Gigi parked the car next to one of the buildings, and they all got out and went inside. A man who looked like a cop sat at a big desk that had double doors in the wall to one side. Mama told him their names. In a few minutes, a lady came through the double doors and shook hands with Mama and Gigi. The lady seemed okay, but distant in a way.

"And this is Janis," Mama said, looking down at her.

"Hello, Janis. I'm Dr. Tandy." The lady crouched so that her face was only a little higher than hers.

Seeing a strange grownup at such close range frightened her. She tried to hide behind her mother. But then her brain told her something about the woman. "Your mama didn't love you, either," she blurted.

16

Mama gasped. "That's not true, Janis! You shut up this minute!"

Gigi said nothing at all.

Dr. Tandy glanced up at them, then returned her gaze to Janis. "No, she didn't," she said evenly. "But I've been very happy here. You will be, too." She stood and turned to Mama. "I see what you mean."

Mama laughed, embarrassed. "She's a handful."

"I can imagine. You were right to bring her here." She motioned toward the door she had just come out of. "Let's all go on back and I'll show you around the facility. And then, if everything seems suitable, we'll get started."

Mama nodded. Gigi's expression was set as hard as concrete.

Dr. Tandy took Janis's hand. "I can tell already," she told the little girl, "that you and I are going to be very good friends."

Chapter 4 — Seven years later

"Who wants to come up and write their homework answers on the board?" Ms. Osterreich invited. The usual kids raised their hands, but she didn't call on them. As always, she was looking for someone she could embarrass in front of the whole class.

Jan sunk lower in his seat, hoping she wouldn't pick on him. So of course she did.

"Jan!" she called. "Come on up!"

Gloomily, he swept his fine brown hair out of his eyes and grabbed his worksheet as he slid out of his seat. His hair fell right back into its accustomed position as he made his way to the front of the room, just as he'd known it would.

"You only need to do the first one," Ms. Osterreich encouraged him. "Then it will be someone else's turn."

He nodded, picked up a stick of chalk, and turned to the board. He spent a great deal of time drawing the division sign: a line level with the horizon, with a hook dangling off the left side. He lavished the same care on the 360 that went just below the line. As he nestled the 9 into the crook of the hook, he heard the telltale sounds of distraction behind him: papers rustling, feet shifting on the floor. Somebody dropped a pencil. As if that was his cue, he hurriedly wrote 40 above the line, slammed the chalk down so hard it broke, and dashed for his seat.

"Jan!" Ms. Osterreich called.

He froze, hands on the front of his desk and butt halfway down. He looked up at her, all innocence, and said, "The answer's right, isn't it?"

"Yes," she said. "But you didn't show your work."

He stared at her as if she were mad. Undaunted, she held out a broken piece of chalk.

Someone a couple of rows over giggled.

He sighed and straightened laboriously. He left his worksheet at his desk; there was no help for him there. He hadn't shown his work on any of the problems.

He took the chalk from Ms. Osterreich and went to the board. There, he stared at the problem, trying to remember how he would get the answer if he had to do it the hard way.

"The 9 goes into…" Ms. Osterreich prompted.

Right. The 9 goes into something and it makes the 4 on top. He thought some more. *It wouldn't be 3. There's not enough room for 9 in a 3. It must be the 6 – but then what happens to the 3?* "Wait," he muttered. In a burst of inspiration, he wrote 360 under the original 360, drew another horizontal line under that, and put a zero below the whole thing. He turned to his teacher, triumphant.

She shook her head. Then she erased the zero in the 360 on the bottom and wrote two more zeroes in a vertical row under the one he'd made, with another horizontal line in between them. Two dashes – *minus signs,* he realized miserably – completed the display. She shot him an unreadable glance, then turned away. "Thank you, Jan. Britt? Please come up and do problem two."

"Aw, man," Britt complained, drawing laughter. Jan was glad of it. It covered his ignominious trip back to his seat.

Britt showed his work the first time, although his answer was wrong. Ms. Osterreich was a lot more cheerful when she showed him his mistake.

She picked on another couple of kids. Then she had everyone pass their worksheets to the front, where she collected them. She began explaining what to do if you had two numbers to the left of the hook instead of just one. Jan listened for a few minutes, but then tuned her out. He hated long division. All this effort to show how you got your answer. What difference did it make, as long as the answer was right? And his answers always were. It was as if he had access to the answers in his head – just by looking at a problem, he saw what needed to go in the blank.

It was the same in every subject. He never had to think through a question. He always just knew the answer. As long as nobody asked him how he got to it, everything was fine.

Language Arts was worse. When Ms. Osterreich had them make up a story, he never knew what to write about. There was no right answer for him to give – anything he wrote would be equally right. Or wrong.

Numbers made more sense to him. As long as nobody asked him how he got his answers.

The lunch bell rang, and Jan and his classmates began lining up at the door to head to the cafeteria. He averted his eyes as he passed Ms. Osterreich's desk – *you don't see me, you don't hear me* – but his impromptu incantation didn't work. She called him over anyway.

She had pulled his worksheet out of the pile and pushed it toward him. "You didn't show your work on any of these problems," she said. "You didn't even write down the ones we did together in class."

"My answers are right, aren't they?" he said, grasping at a straw.

"They are, but…" She looked at him very seriously. "There's more to math than just getting the answer. Math teaches you reasoning skills."

He was silent. He didn't know what she meant by that.

"And your short essay answers on the Social Studies test we took on Monday," she said. "It almost seemed like you were reading my answer key and writing down whatever was in there. But that would be impossible."

His eyes widened. "There's an answer key?" *That explains a lot. I didn't know where the words were coming from.*

Ms. Osterreich sighed. "Parent-teacher conferences are next week. Are your parents planning to come? I'd like to talk with them."

"But I get all the answers right!" he protested, pushing his bangs out of his eyes again.

"You're not in trouble, Jan," she said gently. "I just want to discuss something with your parents."

He stared at his feet, his bangs falling forward again. "They won't listen. They'll just send me to therapy again." He looked up at her through his hair. "That's their answer to everything. Enrichment classes and therapy."

He saw pity in her gaze. "I don't believe you need therapy," she said.

"Good. Can I go to lunch now?"

"Of course." She smiled brightly and turned back to her desk.

And as he trudged out the door, he saw his future tumble into place: his parents coming home from their meeting with Ms. Osterreich; his mother dabbing at her nose as she packed his travel duffel and the backpack with the dumb teddy bear on it; a tall, wrought-iron gate swinging open to reveal a bunch of low buildings, set amidst grass and trees; and a blond-haired girl he'd never seen before, turning to give him the oddest look. As if she knew him, inside and out.

Everything happened just as he'd known it would – although as usual, he had missed some details. His parents had a fight after they met with his teacher. He could hear their raised voices coming from behind the closed door of their bedroom, long after he was supposed to be asleep.

His second-grade teacher had called it a learning disability. His third-grade teacher had suggested he be tested for ADHD, whatever that was. Now he was in fourth grade, and Ms. Osterreich must have come up with yet another diagnosis.

Every time his parents received a new report on the trouble he had in school, they dutifully followed the teacher's recommendations, trotting him around to specialist after specialist. Cost was not an issue, his father always said. After all, he made good money. He and his wife would do anything for Jan. He was their only child. All they wanted was for him to be perfect.

Jan was pretty sure he would never be perfect.

The day came at last when the wrought-iron gates loomed before him. His father drove right up to them, rolled down his window, and barked into a box on a short pole in front of the gate. It swung open and they drove in, past the trees and rolling lawns.

He shook hands with the woman in the blue lab coat with "Dr. Tandy" embroidered on one side. He hardly heard his father clear his throat and tell him to be a good boy; he hardly noticed his red-rimmed eyes. He suffered through his mother's too-tight hug and her promise that they would all be together again at Thanksgiving.

At last they parted. He could not stay to wave goodbye to his parents through the plate-glass windows that rimmed the lobby. Instead, he ran ahead of Dr. Tandy to the big door and pushed it open. He was on fire to see the girl from his vision.

There she was, just as he knew she would be. Her long blond hair swung in an arc around her shoulders as she turned to him. It wafted into place as she regarded him sadly. "Hello," she said. "I'm sorry."

"Sorry?" he said. "For what?"

"For you. You really do love them, but you'll never see them again."

"You're wrong," he said. "My mom said..."

She shook her head. "Choices have consequences," she said. "Your parents chose to put you here. They know what that means. And *you* have chosen to love them anyway. Now you have to suffer the consequences of your choice."

"What consequences?" he said, scoffing.

She turned away. "Everyone has their heart torn out eventually. Your turn is coming sooner than most."

"You're wrong!" He grabbed her shoulder and forced him to turn back to him. "Anyway, how would *you* know?"

22

"I know everything about you," she said. "You have a great gift. So do I, but mine's different than yours. I see the past, but *you* see the future."

"Yeah, well, what *I* see is a crazy girl who thinks my parents hate me!" But even as he spoke, he could see an endless parade of days rolling out before him, and every one of them was spent here. With this girl.

A girl whose words were tearing out his heart.

Chapter 5 — Four years later

Jan took off his headphones and slammed them on the desk in disgust. "I can't!"

In the glass-enclosed booth in front of him, Dr. Tandy leaned toward a microphone on a long, flexible stalk. The intercom in his testing room squawked to life. "Try again, please, Jan."

"No!" he yelled into his own microphone. The recording tech in the booth winced and moved his own headphones partway off his ears. Jan took vicious glee in the man's pain. "I've *told* you — it doesn't work the way you think it does. I can't turn the Sight on and off like a faucet or something."

"Not now, you can't," Dr. Tandy said soothingly. "But with practice and training…"

"That's not how it works!" he yelled, interrupting her. "You don't understand!"

She and the recording tech exchanged a look. Then she got back on the mic. "Maybe we should take a break."

"Yeah, let's," Jan growled, and ran for the door. He yanked it open and walked out into the hallway, nearly colliding with Janis.

"Hey, whoa," she said, stepping back.

"Sorry. I just…"

She tilted her head. "Tandy's getting to you?"

His hands balled into fists of their own accord. "She just doesn't get how I See stuff. My talent doesn't work like yours does. I can't just call it up." He tossed his head, a habitual gesture that sometimes worked to get his hair out of his eyes.

"I can't just call mine up, either."

"But you get better results!"

She rolled her eyes. "It's not a contest!"

Jan shoved his fists in his pockets. "Yeah, it is." He leaned toward her. "Don't tell me you haven't noticed it. They've been trying to pit us against each other for weeks."

She nodded slowly. "You're right. There have been a bunch of times lately when Tandy told me you'd done better than me on this or that test. Like it would make me want to beat you. I bet she was telling you the same thing."

"We should start keeping track," he said. "I'll make a chart this afternoon. We can update it every day after dinner."

"Okay."

Their plan went off without a hitch. They were in the habit of doing homework together in the evenings anyway. They always sat next to each other at the table in the lounge area that adjoined their bedrooms. It was simple enough to incorporate the practice of passing the paper chart back and forth, covered by their other assignments.

The pattern became apparent almost immediately; after a couple of weeks, it was unmistakable. "Tandy really is trying to get us to compete," Janis said one evening as she filled in details of her afternoon session.

The tests they underwent varied somewhat in the details from day to day, but the goal was always the same: to explore the range of their abilities. In Jan's case, Dr. Tandy and the other researchers wanted to know how far into the future he could See, and whether he ever saw more than one possible future track. With Janis, they seemed to be more interested in the level of detail in her visions, and whether her rational or emotional side was most impacted by what she learned. For both children, the researchers wanted to learn what triggered their abilities. More than once, they were presented with a puzzle similar to an earlier trigger, to determine whether it would work again.

"Why, though?" said Janis.

Jan shrugged. "No idea. But here's another thing." He leaned toward her. "Don't you think it's weird that we're the only two kids here?"

She gave him a blank stare. "Weird how?"

He leaned back. "That's right. I always forget you've been here longer than me."

"Nearly all my life," she reminded him.

"I remember *now*," he said, a touch of scorn in his tone. Then he softened. "Well, see, most kids go to school with a lot of other kids. Eighteen or twenty kids in a classroom with one teacher. Lots of classrooms in each school." He thought back. "A lot of kids do stuff with kids their age after school, too. Sports teams, art classes, dance lessons, stuff like that. Or sometimes they just, you know, hang out with the other kids who live in their neighborhood." Suddenly he remembered Tony, who lived two houses away on their cul-de-sac and who had been in all of his classes since second grade. He had liked hanging out with Tony. One summer they built a fort of branches and scrap lumber in the vacant lot behind their subdivision.

He realized with a pang that he missed Tony. He hadn't thought about him in years.

Janis's hand on his ended his reverie. "I'm sure he misses you, too," she said quietly.

Her hand was cool and comforting. He pulled away and said, "See? Your talent comes out so easily."

"It's easiest with people I'm close to," she said. Deliberately, she put her hand back atop his and squeezed his fingers. Then she leaned forward and kissed him on the mouth.

It took him by surprise, but he let her do it. And when she pulled away, he pulled her back for more.

After a minute or two, they parted, their breaths coming fast. Then Janis hurriedly picked up her things and went to her room.

Jan watched until she closed her door. Then his gaze traveled to the gray glass dome in a corner of the room. The domes were all over the building. They had long since figured out that each one concealed a security camera. "I hope you got all that," he muttered to whoever was assigned to watch them that night. Then he sighed, picked up his own

26

things, and headed toward his room, on the opposite side of the lounge from hers.

Janis could not get to sleep that night. Her thoughts ping-ponged from one uncomfortable topic to another. Why had she kissed Jan? She knew he was still hurting from his parents' abandonment, and she had Seen how deep his feelings ran for the kid who lived down the street. She wanted to make him feel better. She didn't want him to hurt so badly. She wanted to help him. But why *kiss* him?

His pain had cracked open her own longing for love, and now it was seeping blood. Soon it would be a torrent. And she didn't know how to make it stop.

She knew it was partly due to the awkward situation they were living in. Jan was right – most kids didn't live the way they did, paired off from childhood and forced to do everything together. The two of them had all their classes together. They ate all their meals together. They were each others' only support. Oh, the Institute provided them with adult supervision – tutors, medical personnel, security guards, and of course Dr. Tandy, who wanted to know everything about their Sight – but it's not like either one of them had ever had someone to rock them to sleep at night.

Jan had once told Janis about the time he'd been sick with a fever. His mother had sat with him and read him picture books endlessly. And that night, when he couldn't sleep, she had held him in her lap and sung to him until he closed his eyes.

Janis had tried – and failed – to picture her mother being so kind and caring. Gigi might have done it, but not Mama.

Honestly, she never wanted to see her mother again. The only thing that woman had left her with was a broken promise and this deep ache inside her.

Why had she kissed Jan?

She turned to face the wall and forced herself to think about something else. Like the tests the two of them kept having to undergo. What were those for? She was incapable of believing there was anything altruistic behind it; Dr. Tandy and the rest weren't interested only in helping her and Jan grow into their talents. No, there had to be another reason.

Then she remembered hearing that sometimes people liked to compete against each other – that it encouraged them to stretch themselves and do better than they would have without that push. Maybe that's what Tandy was up to. But then why not just outright tell them she was making it a contest? Why play mind games with them?

Although everything Tandy ever did to them was a mind game, when it came right down to it.

Sometimes she wished she had Jan's ability instead of her own. If she could see the future, she might get answers to the swarm of questions that always hovered in the back of her mind: What did these people want with her? Would she ever leave the Institute? Would Jan be with her? Or would he leave her with another aching hole in her chest?

Why had she *kissed* him?

She dawdled the next morning, waiting until nearly the last minute to emerge from her room and grab breakfast before class. She hoped to miss him.

Of course, he used the same strategy. They tripped over each other several times in their haste to pour themselves cereal and milk in the tiny kitchen just off the lounge. Janis ate so fast that she dribbled milk on her shirt. Her exclamation of annoyance got Jan's attention, but his gaze strayed to her shirt and stayed there. Her face flamed, and she fled back to her room to change.

Class time was mostly fine, although she avoided looking at him. They always ate lunch at different times because of the testing sessions, so that was okay. But Janis couldn't concentrate during her session – her thoughts kept straying to dinner, when she would see him again.

He was there before her, his dinner half eaten before she could heat hers in the microwave. As she emerged from the kitchen with her tray, she sucked in a breath and pasted on a mocking smile, as if last night had never happened. "You could have waited for me," she said. "Were you starving or something?"

"You should have been more prompt," he returned with a lopsided grin. Then he flipped a silver coin at her.

She caught it before it fell into her mashed potatoes. "Hey!"

"Look at it," he urged, all traces of humor gone.

She studied it. On one side was the logo for the Institute. On the opposite side was a head with two faces, as if one had been grafted onto the back of the other's head. A couple of branches framed the heads on either side. "What is this?" she asked, turning the coin over and over.

"I went wandering the halls this afternoon," he said. "There's a room where they were setting up for something. A meeting or a party, maybe. I don't know. But they had these scattered all over the tables."

"Okay," she said slowly. "And?"

He pointed at the two-faced figure. "I found the image in my history book," he said. "It's Janus, the Roman god of gates and doors."

She squinted up at him. "I'm named after a Roman god?"

"Not exactly. The Romans spelled it J-A-N-U-S," he clarified.

"Oh, okay," she said. "What's with the two heads, though?"

"One faces the past," he said. "And one faces the future."

One eyebrow went up. "So we're Janus?"

"*Together*, we're Janus. Without each other, we're just two kids with weird abilities."

"But what does that mean?" she asked. "For us, I mean."

"I don't know," he said. "Yet. But that party would be a good place to start looking."

She nodded. "Makes sense. All we need to do is figure out how to get in."

"Leave that to me," he said.

Chapter 6

When Jan had shown Janis the coin and suggested crashing the party or whatever it was going to be, he had projected calm confidence on purpose. Inside, though, he was terrified.

For one thing, he had no idea how he was going to get them into the event. It's not like Dr. Tandy wouldn't spot them – assuming she would be there at all. And then there was the little matter of the security cameras all over the building. Once they realized what the dome in the lounge was for, they began to notice them everywhere: the corridors, their classrooms, and the testing rooms. There were even cameras on the building's exterior, tracking them when the staff allowed them out for exercise. The only place they had any privacy at all was in their own rooms.

As far as he could tell, anyway. If there were cameras in his bedroom or bathroom, he wasn't adept enough to figure out where they were.

If their plan was going to have any chance of succeeding, they would have to figure out how to disable the cameras – or else distract whoever was keeping an eye on them. And there wasn't much time to figure it all out.

That wasn't the only thing that terrified him, though. The other thing was Janis.

He had tossed and turned the night before, reliving the kiss she had given him and asking himself why. A year or two before, their science tutor had explained puberty to them – in dry, clinical terms – so when Janis's body began to change, he knew what was happening to her. That her changes would affect *him* so profoundly had never crossed his mind.

The same tutor made sure they were versed in the mechanics of the sex act. But besides that, he'd also gone into a lengthy explanation of maternal nurturing and how critical it was for parents and their children to bond. For days after that session, Janis had brooded. It took time for him to realize she was weighing the nurturing her own mother had given her, and realizing how inadequate it had been. His own mother hadn't been a rock-solid presence in his life – his father's regard had been far more important to him – but at least she'd been there. At least she'd gone to bat for him against teachers and therapists and even, occasionally, against his father. Janis had never had anyone like that in her life; her mother had dumped her here the first chance she got.

He could forgive his parents for leaving him here; he knew they loved him, but both he and they had been ready for a drastic solution. Janis could not forgive her mother.

And now she had kissed him. He didn't know what that meant. And for some reason, it scared him.

He had been chewing on that fear when he started walking – no, running – around the facility, trying to distract himself with physical exertion. That's when he stumbled on the gaily-decorated room with the coins strewn around. There were hundreds if not thousands of them on the tables, so he palmed two and went on his way. But now he had something new to chew over: how to get the two of them into the party, or at least close enough so they could find out what was going on.

As it turned out, he didn't have to rewire any security cameras or bribe any guards. That morning, Dr. Tandy came to the lounge while he and Janis were still at breakfast. She wore a pink lab coat that day, and carried two large packages. "Hello, children," she said.

"Hello," they chorused dutifully. Tandy was no favorite. Sometimes Jan wondered why Janis had never bonded with her – she was so young when she arrived and her mother was so awful – but then he would remember Tandy's chilly personality.

"I have a surprise for you," she said with her mechanical smile. "Some friends of the Institute are coming by this afternoon for a... party, you might call it. We would like you two to attend."

"Do we have to?" Jan said immediately. Out of the corner of his eye, he saw Janis glance at him. He could tell she was surprised, but she covered it immediately. He didn't think Tandy had seen it.

Tandy's smile grew brittle. "Yes, you do."

He crossed his arms and slumped back in his chair.

She went on, speaking now to Janis and ignoring him. "The party begins at four p.m. I've brought outfits for each of you. They're dressier than your usual clothing because there will be important adults at this event – that is, this *party* – and we want you to look your best."

Janis shrugged. "Okay."

"Good." She handed out the packages. "Because of this special event, we'll be cutting our usual afternoon testing sessions short. Each of your will have an hour – Janis at 1:00 p.m. and Jan at 2:00 p.m. But everything will be back to normal tomorrow." She smiled again. "Well, I'll see you this afternoon."

"Yep, see ya," Janis said, peeking into her package. That seemed to be Tandy's cue; she turned on her heel and strode out of the room.

"Thank goodness for small blessings," muttered Jan as soon as the door was shut behind her.

"It's a dress!" Janis cried, delighted. "With heels!" She pulled out a pair of shoes with heels that were indeed higher, although not by much, than the sneakers she usually wore.

Curious, Jan glanced into his package. It contained a navy-blue jacket with matching slacks, a white shirt that buttoned all the way up to the neckline, a red-and-blue-striped tie, and black leather shoes. "This solves one problem," he said. "We don't have to figure out how we're going to get into the party."

"That's right!" Janis said, holding the dress to her chest with one arm. "We have an invitation!"

Janis was dazzled. She had never been to anything so fancy in her life.

Jan had told her the coins featuring the two-headed Roman god had been placed on tables. But he hadn't mentioned how big the room was, or how many tables there were. This room was several times the size of the lounge in their quarters. Tiny tables, much too tall for regular chairs, crowded around the long sides of the room. Each of these small tables had coins scattered across them. Just inside the doors, heaps of coins surrounded a vase of flowers on a rectangular table that also held name tags and a stack of brochures. Every table was swathed in cloth of a rich blue.

At the far end of the room was an elevated platform. On the wall behind it hung a curtain in the same deep blue as the tablecloths, and from that fabric had been hung a blown-up version of the coin, alongside a similarly large-scale reproduction of the Institute's logo. To one side, several musicians played. Their music competed with the murmur of conversation as well as the clink of glassware from the bar along the back wall.

The children hung back by the door. Tandy hadn't told them what to do or where to stand, Janis realized; she'd only said they needed to be there. All at once, it was too much for her: the noise, the unfamiliar surroundings, and the uncertainty. Unconsciously, she sought Jan's hand and held it tightly.

"How many people do you think are here?" he said quietly.

"Too many," she replied, her voice shaky.

He glanced at her. "I know," he said. "I don't like crowds, either. Look, why don't you stand over here next to the door? I'll go up to the table and ask them what we need to do."

She let go of his hand reluctantly and shrank back against the wall while Jan ran the errand for them. She would have made a break for the door if Jan hadn't admitted he didn't like it here, either. She refused to abandon him.

A woman in a slinky, sequined white dress walked past her. The sequins caught her eye – so sparkly! – and then she saw the woman's expression, and everything tumbled into place: she had had a cultured and comfortable upbringing, then maneuvered herself into marriage with a rich man who was much older than her. The man provided her with the lifestyle she had grown up accustomed to, but no one – not her parents and not her husband – had ever given her love.

"Isn't it past your bedtime, little girl?" the woman asked with a sly, unkind look.

"He'll never love you, you know," Janis returned in a matter-of-fact tone. "Not the way you want to be loved."

The sneer froze on the woman's lips.

"I'm sorry," Janis whispered, and she was. Not for telling the truth – the woman already knew it, she was sure – but for the ruin that her life had become. "I'm sorry you chose so poorly."

The woman drew back as if she'd been slapped – or as if she might slap Janis. Then she collected herself. "Harry?" she called, looking around. "I need another drink." She flung a look of contempt at the girl as she slinked away.

"What was that all about?" Jan asked.

"Oh, there you are," said Janis, nearly sagging against him in relief. She looked after the woman. "I told her I was sorry she'd made bad choices in her life. I think she was going to hit me."

"She'd be even more sorry if she did. It looks like we're the main attraction."

"What?"

Jan showed her a printed sheet of paper. "This is the program for tonight – the order in which stuff is supposed to happen. It says Tandy's going to say some stuff, and then show a video, and then introduce us."

Janis's eyes widened. "We aren't going to have to say anything, are we? Or perform like trained seals?"

"I sure hope not," he said.

"Ah, there you are!" a familiar and not particularly well-liked voice said. Sure enough, it was Dr. Tandy. She had abandoned her usual lab

35

coat in favor of a blue-and-silver dress with heels that were much higher than Janis's. She had done up her hair, and a strand of pearls encircled her throat. "My, don't you two look marvelous."

"You look nice, too, Dr. Tandy," Jan said politely.

"I hardly recognized you without your lab coat," Janis said, more honestly.

Tandy didn't bat an eye. "Go ahead and get yourselves a soda," she said, indicating the bar. "Don't ask for anything stronger – the bartenders know you're under age. Then meet me behind the stage. I've arranged for a place for you to sit and wait until it's your turn to go onstage. Oh, good," she said to Jan. "You have a program."

"I'd like one, too," Janis said.

"Of course. You may take one after you get your soda." Dr. Tandy gave her the usual mechanical smile, and then left them to greet the guests.

"Come on," Jan said, nudging her with his elbow. "I want to be in place before this thing starts."

Janis preceded him to the bar, but tracked Tandy's progress. "I hope she doesn't run into Sequin Lady," she said.

"What if she does? All you did was tell her the truth."

"I know. But I'm not sure I want it to get back to Tandy."

Jan laughed.

It turned out the curtain wasn't hung on the back wall, but on a frame attached to the back of the stage. There was a gap between the frame and the wall, and the blue curtain wrapped around the side to shield the backstage area from view. Jan held the curtain back so Janis could duck under it.

It was tight quarters back there, and hot. Cables stretched everywhere, and on the far side of the enclosure, a tech she recognized sat in front of a computer. He waved at them and turned back to his monitor.

36

Two chairs were placed near where they had come in. "I guess these are for us," Jan said, and took one. Janis sat in the other chair and sipped her drink. It didn't seem to want to sit still in her belly, though, so she put her glass on the floor.

"Nervous?" Jan asked.

She nodded. "You?"

"Yeah. I wish I knew what this was all about."

They found out as soon as Tandy began speaking. Her voice was a little muffled because of the curtain, but Janis could still understand her. "Ladies and gentlemen," she said. And again, "Ladies and gentlemen," in a slightly louder tone of voice. The conversational hubbub subsided, and Tandy went on. "Thank you all so very much for being here, and for your past generous support of the Institute. We have two exciting pieces of news for you tonight.

"The first is an update on our mission. As you know, our aim here at the Institute has been to develop methods of discovering the best ways to encourage progress in our world. Right now, the world is flying blind. Researchers and pollsters crunch their numbers and experts in their think tanks give us their best predictions – but they're all just guessing. They are educated guesses, to be sure. But they don't know for sure.

"No one knows anything for sure. We study these educated guesses, many of which conflict with one another, and pick the one our gut tells us is the best. And we hope we're right. But a lot of the time, we're wrong. Then we suffer, and the world suffers, too.

"Here at the Institute, we are working to improve your odds. And tonight, we'd like to tell you about one of our most promising projects. We call it the Dominion Project."

The lights in the room dimmed. The glow from the monitor in the corner was the brightest spot in the room; the tech moved his mouse and clicked it a few times, and a video began showing on the fabric curtain in front of them. The curtain was too thick for Janis to make out details, but she could hear the audio well enough.

An unfamiliar voice began to spin a yarn about this Dominion Project – about how children with paranormal abilities were being trained to improve them in order to use them for the greater good of all humankind.

Then the voice changed to Tandy's. She talked about how rewarding it was for her to work with these exceptional children, to shape their minds and help them reach their full potential.

Then Janis drew in a breath, for the next voice was her own, although she had been much younger when the recording had been made. She remembered the session, of course – she had begun talking about a man who had lived under the highway underpass with Mama and her, and then her Sight took over and she began relating details of his past life. He had grown up in a bad neighborhood in Los Angeles and had joined the military to get out and see the world. What he saw was combat – several tours in Iraq. On his last deployment he'd lost a leg to a land mine. The VA helped him, but he didn't think they'd helped him enough.

"Mama always said Roscoe chose to live that way," Janis said on the tape. "She told me choices have con… consequences."

Jan leaned toward her. "Did you know she was taping you?"

Janis shrugged. "Maybe? I was just a little kid. I think she taped everything when I first got here."

Then it was Jan's turn. This was also an old tape. He explained his teachers didn't like him because he knew all the answers but couldn't tell them how he got them. With Tandy prompting him, Jan finally admitted that he always used his Sight to see the test returned to him with the answers written on it.

"Do you know why you're here?" Tandy asked him on the video.

"Yeah," he said. "Ms. Osterreich wanted to get rid of me, so she told my parents about this place. But that's okay," he went on. "She wasn't going to be my teacher for very much longer anyway."

"Oh? How do you know that?"

"Because I Saw it," he said in a confiding tone. "Her mom's going to get really sick and she's going to leave to take care of her."

"Will her mom get better?" Tandy asked.

"Not before the end of the school year," young Jan said confidently. "So I'd be somebody else's headache."

Janis heard chuckles from the party attendees. She leaned toward Jan. "Did you…?"

"I think so. That was right after I got here. Like you said, she taped everything then."

"Maybe she still does. Maybe she's using a hidden camera."

He nodded, thinking of the dome in the corner of their lounge.

The video had ended and the lights had come back up. Live-action Tandy was back onstage, saying, "Would you like to meet the amazing young people you just saw?"

A smattering of applause. Tandy took that as a yes. "Children, would you please come out here?"

So they did. The applause was louder as they mounted the stage. Janis forced herself to smile at the assembly.

"Thank you, children," Tandy said as the applause died down – obviously their cue to leave.

Janis stepped down first and into the shadow on the side of the stage. She raised the side curtain to duck back under it, but Jan put his hand on her shoulder. He leaned close and said in her ear, "If we stand here, we can hear better."

He was right, she realized. So they stayed right there through Tandy's brief announcement of the second exciting development, which was apparently going to take a lot of money. "We can take credit cards, if you'd like to increase your investment tonight," she said, "or you can wire us the funds as you have in the past. Please take a copy of our annual report from the table, if you haven't already. All the information you will need to make your investment is there.

"That concludes our program. If you have questions, I would be happy to answer them individually. And again, thank you all for coming."

Jan raised the curtain and ducked back under it. Janis followed him. "Do we need to stay?" she asked.

"No idea. But I don't want to walk through that crowd, now that they know who we are."

Janis nodded and took her seat again. She finished her soda and began rolling the program into a tube, first one way and then the other. Jan paced back and forth between his chair and the curtain.

They could hear the room empty out. When it was quiet, the tech shut down his computer, then stood and stretched. "You two should probably get going."

Just then Tandy ducked her head through the curtain. "You're still here? I thought I had made it clear you could go back to your rooms."

"No, ma'am, you hadn't," Jan said.

She seemed annoyed. "Well, go on. I will see you in the morning." She held the curtain open for them.

The children traded a glance and did as they were told.

Back in their own quarters, dinner was waiting for them. As they sat down to eat, Janis said, "What was that all about, anyway?"

Jan shrugged. "I don't know. But I know one thing for sure."

"What's that?"

He nodded toward the dome in the corner. "I'm going to keep a better eye out for hidden cameras from now on."

New Mexico

Chapter 7

Jan stood, speechless, his arms around Janis for the first time in forty years. He had so much to say to her – so much to explain about what was coming – but all he could do was stand there and hold her.

She was different, and yet the same. She looked like somebody's maiden aunt, all schoolmarm-like, with her baby blue cardigan and cat's-eye reading glasses, and the bun on top of her head. She had been a lot thinner when they parted, but he had been thinner then, too. And anyway, that hardly mattered. She was still the Janis he remembered, in all the ways that counted. He could sense the core of her, still as hard and inflexible as it had been the first day they met, when she told him he'd never see his parents again.

She had been wrong about that, in a way. But then, reading the future was *his* talent.

"I bet you're hell on your students," he blurted.

She laughed. "Only the ones who give me a hard time."

He chuckled, and at last stepped back.

She looked up at him with eyes that were warm but wary. "I'd ask why you're here, but I can guess the answer to that," she said. "I suppose the devil is in the details."

He blew out a breath. "Yeah. We have a lot to talk about."

"No doubt."

He looked around the cramped office. A large desk took up most of the real estate, while a bookshelf and a side chair, both stacked haphazardly with books and folders, fought with a four-drawer filing cabinet for the rest of it. A couple of items with the school's emblem dotted the shelves. A plant with spindly runners overspread the top of the filing cabinet. The top of her desk was pristine. "Can we talk here, now? Or do you have to go back to work?"

She wrinkled her nose in chagrin. "I probably should. This is the last period of day – I'll be free in forty-five minutes, and then we can go somewhere more comfortable. You're welcome to stay here and wait. That is, unless you have to be somewhere."

"No," he said quickly. "No. There's nowhere else I need to be."

She smiled in relief. "Make yourself comfortable, then – if you can. There's tea in the bottom drawer, and one of those little immersible water heaters that would get me fired if the janitor ever found out I had it."

He laughed again. "I'll never tell." His eyes softened. "I guess I can wait another forty-five minutes."

She put a hand on his chest. Then she brushed past him and went back out into the main part of the library.

He shut the door and leaned against it. Then he closed his eyes and tried to will his Sight to work. He tried every trick he knew to get the future to tumble out before his mind's eye.

Ten minutes later, he gave up. He was simply not going to receive any further clues about what the future held for Janis and him.

He sighed and pushed away from the door. It was probably just as well. If the news were terrible, he wouldn't want to know, anyway.

He took the step and a half from the door to the desk chair and sat down. He resisted an urge to rifle through her drawers – not to look for contraband, but to see what sort of person she had become. The top of her desk gave him no clues at all. There were no photos on display – no family, no pets, not even a shot from some vacation spot. She had a computer, of course, and a plain white mug full of pencils and pens, but that was it.

It occurred to him that his desk at work was the same way.

She must have been hiding in plain sight, too, all this time.

He rose rapidly from the chair and took the half-step to the filing cabinet. He found himself examining the wan plant. It probably needed

44

more light, he thought. The office had no windows. It was probably too dark on weekends and school holidays.

He checked his wristwatch for the time, scratched his head, and went out into the library.

Janis, at the circulation desk next to her student assistant, quirked an eyebrow at him. "I'd like to borrow a book," he said.

"You're in luck. We happen to have some," she said. "Fiction or nonfiction?"

"I'll just browse, if that's okay."

"Of course." And she turned back to her work. A passerby would think she was instantly engrossed in whatever she was working on, but he saw the familiar quirk of her lips.

With a small smile of his own, he stepped away and began browsing the stacks. He was still looking when the final bell rang.

Janis joined him shortly after the final student left. "You still haven't found anything?"

"It appears I've read all of them." He grinned at her.

"Mrs. Fowler?" a voice called from the doorway. They both turned to see the student who had been working with Janis at the desk. "Oh, good, you're still here," she said in relief. "I forgot my astronomy book behind the desk, and we have a test tomorrow." She retrieved the book and waved. "Goodnight!"

"Goodnight, Teresa," Janis called pleasantly. Then she turned back to him.

"*Mrs.* Fowler?" he asked.

She cocked her head playfully. "Jealous?"

"I haven't decided yet. I'm still trying to figure out why a woman would use Mrs. with her maiden name."

"There's a lot you don't know about me," she said. "Come on. Let's go to my place." She paused, then added quickly, "To talk, of course. Unless you'd rather get dinner. But it's kind of early for that, and…"

45

His booming laugh cut her short. "Let's just get out of here. Your place is fine."

Chapter 8

"So what's this all about?" Janis asked, once they were settled with beverages in her living room. She was glad she had taken the extra few minutes to straighten up and run the dishwasher before she'd left for work. She had been letting those little chores slide too often lately. It was tempting to blame old age, but knew that wasn't the whole reason. Besides, she told herself, she wasn't that old.

Jan grinned engagingly. "Can't a fellow look up an old friend?"

She waited, giving him the no-bull-hockey look that had cowed several generations of high schoolers.

He was still smiling, but less mischievously. "It was worth a try."

"That's what they all say." But she relaxed her expression to one of expectant interest.

"Okay." He set down his glass. He had opted for ice water; she had gone for tea. "I'm a senior project manager for Jemez Aerospace. That's a government contractor in Los Alamos."

She nearly dropped her cup. "You're in Los Alamos? How long have you lived there?"

"Almost forty years," he said.

She had been in Santa Fe for nearly as long. "So close," she said softly. "For all this time."

They were both silent for a moment, Janis thinking about coincidences. They had ended up settling down just thirty-five miles from each other. She had been to Los Alamos a few times over the years for conferences and the like. She might have walked past him and never realized it.

Maybe it hadn't been a coincidence, though. Maybe their respective talents had been in communion all this time, keeping tabs, keeping the other one nearby. So all would be in readiness when it was time.

Jan cleared his throat and took a sip of water. "Well," he began again. "Last Friday, as I was about to leave the office for the day, I received an email about a new client we were about to bring on board. That is, the email went to everyone in the office – it's just that I was the only person still there. Everybody else read it Monday morning.

"Anyway, the client is involved in a project we've been working on for NASA."

"Is this the Mars mission?" she asked.

He blinked. "*You're* up-to-date."

She laughed. "Not normally. I just happen to know about it because one of our alumni is going to be aboard the spaceship. Rocket. Whatever."

"*Spacecraft* is the word you're looking for," he said, his mouth turning up at the corners.

"Spacecraft," she amended. "Anyway. Joe Bitsuie graduated from El Camino Real High about ten years ago. He came by last month to talk about the mission and about careers at NASA in general. There was an assembly for the whole school, and then I think he met with the kids taking upper-level math and science courses. Nice guy. Of course he got into his share of scrapes when he was a student, but he seems to have straightened himself out." She smiled, remembering young Joe.

"Did you know him when he a student there?"

"Oh, sure. I didn't work with him – library aides tend to be bookworms and Joe was definitely not – but everybody ends up in the library for classwork sooner or later." She sipped her tea. "So anyway, your new client."

"Right. So there I was, debating whether to read the email or leave it for Monday."

"And you opened it."

"And I opened it. Could not leave well enough alone." He grinned again. Then his smile faded. "And I read a familiar name – Dr. Denise Tandy."

48

She had expected something like this, but she caught her breath anyway. "The Institute," she said. "They're your new client?"

"They don't call themselves that anymore, but it's pretty clear it's the same outfit. Now it's known as Foundation for the Advancement of Excellence." He eyed her speculatively – waiting for her reaction, she supposed.

"I thought they'd shut down after we left," she said carefully. "That's what I understood, anyway."

"I understood the same thing," he replied.

"I guess they didn't."

"I guess not."

Her hand shook slightly. She put down her cup. "What's their involvement in the Mars mission?"

He shifted in his seat. "Well, as you may know, NASA is doing some preliminary work to discover whether we could set up a colony there one day." He snorted. "Colonizing Mars has been a recurring subject of science fiction stories for probably a hundred years. But the people who do science for a living never thought it would be practical. The only thing Mars really has going for it is its proximity to Earth – other than that, it's a harsh environment. There's no breathable air to speak of, the temperature extremes are unviable – a whole host of complications. But NASA has been given this mandate to put a base on Mars. So we're going." He tipped his water glass toward Janis. "Your former student included."

"He talked about all of that during the assembly," she said. "He told us great strides have been made in tackling all of those problems. That we could have people living there within thirty years."

"That's a little optimistic," he said. "From what I've heard, the timeline is closer to a century. But we have to start somewhere."

"Sure." She thought for a moment. "Did you say your company is a defense contractor?"

"I did." He nodded.

"Then why are you involved with the Mars mission?"

He tapped his temple with a forefinger. "That's an excellent question. The answer is there's a defense component to the mission."

"I see."

"That's not something that's generally known. People feel less threatened when they think about Mars as a site for a civilian colony someday. But when NASA talks about building a base on Mars, what they're really talking about is a military base."

She gave him a dubious look. "What possible use could we have for a military base on another planet? It's too far away to use to shoot a missile at some country we're mad at."

"Of course. But what if an alien race happens to notice that we're sufficiently advanced to have begun colonizing our solar system? It wouldn't make sense to leave those colonists defenseless."

"Hmm." She thought about that for a second. "I suppose that's true. Plus they would have no way of knowing how soon we might start sending colonists farther afield."

"That thought has also occurred to the honchos at NASA."

"So what's the Institute's involvement? Or whatever they're calling themselves these days."

He sat forward, propping his forearms on his knees. "I don't know. I haven't gotten that far in my investigation yet. I wanted to find you first."

"To alert me," she said. "That the time had come for us to be together again."

He nodded, his eyes meeting hers. "Yes. Exactly that." He held her gaze for a long moment, then broke it off. "What's your situation right now?"

"My situation?" she said, flustered by both the long soulgaze and his abrupt change of subject.

"Married? Family? How easy would it be to get away from your job?"

"Oh. Well." She glanced around her living room, as if the answers to his questions were lurking there. "No marriage and no family." She let out a breath. She had kept that secret for such a long time, it felt wrong to voice it now. But she believed she could trust Jan. He might be the only person in the world she could fully trust.

"So why the Mrs., then?" he asked.

She lifted her hands. "It seemed easier. I told everyone I had been married but my husband had been in the military and stationed overseas, where he died tragically." She looked at Jan. "You know, back in the day, employers didn't necessarily want to hire young, single women. They figured they would just about get the girls trained and settled in, and they would up and get married and quit. Or get pregnant and quit. I had no intention of doing either one, but of course you couldn't come right out and say that to a prospective employer – and if you did, they might not believe you anyway. So I told everyone I was a widow, still in mourning for the tragic loss of my sainted husband. Problem solved."

He seemed relieved. "Fair enough. Uh, and the job?"

"That would be trickier," she admitted. "I could take a leave of absence, but they're not always granted, and the approval usually takes a while. Not something I could pull off on the spur of the moment." She looked away. "Although I've been toying with the idea of retiring early. I could just about afford it."

He nodded thoughtfully. "We'll keep that as an option, then. How much notice would you have to give?"

She blinked "I have no idea. I never got that far along with the planning. It was just a thought."

"Okay. Look into it. Just so we have our ducks in a row."

Janis sat up straighter. "Yes, sir."

He laughed ruefully. "Sorry. Didn't mean to make it sound like an order."

She softened. "So what about you? Marriage? Family? And how quickly could you leave *your* job?"

"No and no, to the first two questions," he said. "As far as the guys at work know, I'm a hermit." He chuckled. "There's a rumor going around the office that I'm gay."

"Are you?"

"Nope. But it makes a good cover story when they start talking about getting laid."

She laughed aloud. "You haven't changed a bit!"

"Neither have you," he said.

Another pause while they stared intently at one another. She broke the spell by picking up her tea. It had gone cold, so she took a hearty slug. "And your job?" she went on, as if the atmosphere in the room weren't supercharged. "Could *you* quit at a moment's notice?"

"Two weeks," he said, never taking his eyes off her. "I'd have to give two weeks' notice. Although I'm not planning to quit unless it's absolutely necessary. I'm in a better position to suss out information right now, while working on the project, than I would be on the outside."

"Makes sense," she said. "When will you know more, do you think?"

"There's a meeting scheduled with the client in a couple of days," he said. "I wanted to touch base with you before that happened. Just so you knew."

"Right. Of course. Just so I knew." She finished the tea. It was cold as ice. "Jan."

He regarded her, alert.

"Do you find it funny?" she said. "That neither of us ever married. Or even dated anyone."

"Not funny at all," he said. "I knew what I wanted. I just couldn't have it."

"Yes," she breathed. "Exactly."

He slid down the couch. "I don't know whether I'll have it, even now," he said. "My Sight tells me nothing about our future."

"Don't ask me. Mine only works in the other direction." She reached for his hand and he took it. "I guess we'll just have to play it by ear," she said. "But at least we'll be together."

Chapter 9

Jan tried hard to be the last person to arrive at meetings. It meant he often had a suboptimal seat for seeing the presentation, but it also cut down on time he had to spend socializing with his co-workers.

It wasn't that he was antisocial. It was just easier to keep from blowing his cover if he limited his interactions with other people. The less they knew about his talent, the better off all of them would be.

He had long since given up using his Sight to see the right answers. Somewhere along the way, he'd figured out that it was better to do his own thinking than to just regurgitate what others wanted him to say. Come to think of it, he probably had the Institute to thank for that.

He had spent the past four decades hiding from the Institute. Now, today, they were going to show up on his home turf. It would be a lousy day to give up his usual habit.

So at about ten seconds past 10:00 a.m., he quietly opened the door to the firm's biggest conference room and found a seat way in the back corner. His buddy and supervisor, Dan Abioye, didn't notice his slightly tardy arrival – he was too busy adjusting the microphone at the podium. Jan noticed the big screen to Dan's right, with his boss's image front and center, and below it, a row of smaller windows featuring live video from the firm's other offices: New York, Silicon Valley, Beijing, and Amsterdam. "The gang's all here," he muttered to himself.

"Good morning, everyone," Dan said. "Or I guess it's afternoon in New York and early evening in Europe. And who knows what time it is in Asia." He grinned at his own joke. "We wanted to take the opportunity today to introduce you to our company's newest client – the Foundation for the Advancement of Excellence – and tell you more about what we will be doing with them. As you know, the FAE has partnered with NASA on Project Terraform, and our work will dovetail with theirs in some important respects. To tell you about that, I'd like to introduce Dr. Denise Tandy, the president and chief executive officer of FAE. Dr. Tandy?"

There was polite applause as two of the video feed windows switched places. Now the Silicon Valley office's window was the largest of the bunch, and the camera zeroed in on a woman taking her place at the podium there.

There was no mistake, even forty years later: This Dr. Tandy was the same woman who haunted Jan in his darkest hours.

The years had been kind to her – or more likely she'd had plastic surgery. No woman in her 80s could be so wrinkle-free without surgical assistance. Her hair was snow white and pulled back into a sleek chignon. At some point she had ditched the ubiquitous lab coat; today she wore a black blouse and slacks, topped by a purple power blazer – the kind with three-quarter-length sleeves with turned-back cuffs. Powerful women wore the style when they wanted men to know they were ready to roll up their sleeves and get down to business.

She was hundreds of miles away. There was no way she could possibly know Jan was in the audience. Regardless, sweat beaded on his brow. He fought an irrational desire to flee.

"Thank you for that warm welcome, Mr. Abioye," Tandy said into the camera, flashing her mechanical smile. "It's good to be here and to meet all of you, if only virtually."

Jan shuddered. Surreptitiously, he leaned closer to the wall next to his chair.

She donned a pair of reading glasses before she went on. "FAE is proud to partner with NASA – as well as with Jemez Aerospace – on Project Terraform. As you know, the administration in Washington is eager to begin working on the Mars colony in earnest. We have all been given our marching orders: a viable colony on the red planet within thirty years." She glanced up from her prepared remarks. "I know some so-called experts believe that goal is unachievable. But I say, what's the point of setting a goal if you're not going to have to stretch yourself to reach it?"

Polite applause greeted her remark.

"I believe it's doable. In fact, I believe that together, we can beat the deadline."

More applause.

"For the past decade, FAE has been working on a top-secret project for the Department of Defense that will help us reach our goal. We have been setting up a team of specialists with rather unusual abilities. Paranormal abilities."

Here it comes, Jan thought, as his colleagues shifted uncomfortably in their seats. He knew a lot of them would consider his own ability as likely as magic.

"Right now, as we speak, we are putting the final touches on a global network of these specialists. Our network will have the ability to sense both military and other types of threats before they happen. It will be able to pinpoint dates and locations for these threats with extreme precision, months before they occur, giving plenty of forewarning to those whose job it is to put a stop to them. That alone makes this effort incredibly valuable.

"But best of all, unlike web-based early-warning systems, our network cannot be hacked. And that's because of what it's made up of. Not computers, not machines – but people."

A buzz of whispers erupted around Jan. He didn't need to eavesdrop on any of these conversations. He knew what they were thinking: Not only is the hint of anything paranormal laughable in connection with what they did, but people are *more* fallible than machines, not less. Maybe the human brain can't be hacked the way a computer network can be, but it's susceptible to reprogramming, delusional thinking, mental illnesses, and on and on. And humans make mistakes all the time.

He agreed with all that – up to a point. But if the abilities of this team of Tandy's were like his and Janis's, then they would indeed be very difficult to hack. Maybe something like a post-hypnotic suggestion could throw a prediction off. But his Sight dealt in facts – not probabilities, even, but certainties: Given the current trajectory of events, A will follow B in precisely this way, and C will be the result. He had sometimes Seen a range of possibilities, but they were typically variations on a theme rather than multiple distinct scenarios. And regardless of the number of variations, events virtually always ended up at the same place.

So he could not scoff at Tandy's claim. For the purposes of her program, humans *weren't* hackable.

Tandy was oblivious to his co-workers' suppressed mirth, however; she plowed on, without even acknowledging the possibility that her premise could be wrong. "You may be asking yourself what this has to do with Project Terraform," she said. "We are excited to announce our plans to extend our project to the new colony on Mars. Once our team is in place there, the ability of the United States to detect and neutralize threats from anywhere – even in space – will be unparalleled. Together with the robust terrestrial and space defenses we already have, the United States will continue to be safe and secure for decades to come."

Jan glanced toward his boss, who sat in the front row. He didn't have a completely clear line of sight, but it appeared to him that Dan hadn't reacted at all to Tandy's preposterous claims. Jan wondered whether Dan had known the details of FAE's project, and what he thought of it. He made a mental note to drop by the boss's office after lunch.

"To give you more details on this remarkable program of ours, I'd like to introduce you now to our vice president of global operations, Antoine Jenkins. Antoine?"

Tandy stepped out of the frame and made way for a young man. He was young – mid-twenties at most – and appeared to be of about average height. His skin was a warm brown and his hair was done in short dreadlocks. He had an engaging smile and seemed completely at ease in front of the camera.

Before the man had even begun to speak, Jan knew what he was going to say. Moreover, he knew everything he would *not* say about FAE's plans, and why. The only thing he didn't know – the one thing his Sight stopped short of showing him – was whether he and Janis would be able to stop FAE before any serious damage could be done.

He realized the room had gone quiet. Many of his co-workers had turned around to stare at him, huddled in his corner against the wall. He wondered why – but then he focused on the screen, where Antoine Jenkins was staring at him through the video connection.

"You," was all he said.

It seemed like a door opened inside Jan's chest. Senses and abilities that he had kept a lid on for forty years sprang to life. Old vows took on new meaning. Long-buried desires for justice burned anew.

Quietly but fiercely, he said, "Good luck. You're going to need it."

He blinked. No one was staring at him, least of all the man on the screen. Tandy's vice president of global operations was going on about his pet project, radiating enthusiasm with his words and gestures, but not really saying much of anything at all. It was as if Antoine Jenkins had never focused on him.

But Jan had no doubt that what he had experienced was real. In those moments of time out of time, a gauntlet had been dropped – and he had picked it up.

Chapter 10

Janis felt Jan's door open.

She was sitting at the information desk in the school library, explaining the rules of research to a sophomore who had apparently never used a computer for anything but RPGs and chatting with friends on Discord, when something sprang free in her own chest. She knew she had bottled up a lot of feelings when she left the Institute, but hers were mostly angry – and sorrowful. She had not gone through what Jan had. Some of what she was feeling now had the flavor of her last interactions with him.

She looked up to see the sophomore staring quizzically at her. "What?" she said, rather crossly.

"I said, 'Are you okay?' "

"Of course! Why wouldn't I be okay?"

"Well," the boy said, "you grabbed the front of your sweater and said something about being...blown?" He wore an innocent look, but she saw the humor lurking in the depths of his eyes.

"What I said was, 'I've got a blow, Jane!'" she returned tartly. "It's a quote from *Jane Eyre* by Charlotte Bronte. In that novel, Mr. Rochester utters those words when Jane gives him some bad news. And I said it because I'm about to give *you* some: you're going to need a more credible source than Wikipedia for this paper."

As the student expostulated about how it wasn't fair that his teacher had banned Wikipedia, she congratulated herself on tying her comment into the conversation so neatly. Then she gave him her rote speech about how you can't believe everything you see on the internet, and sent him back to the computer to find some more credible sources. She lamented privately that the school didn't spend more time on teaching critical thinking – it would make her job much easier. But it was an old internal argument, and she was getting tired of having it. She began to think maybe she *should* retire. She was beginning to lose her zest for the job.

Or maybe it was just that Jan was back in her life.

And that thought reminded her of the blow she had received.

At lunch, she closeted herself in her office and used her cell phone to call him on his. "What happened?" she demanded as soon as he answered.

He sighed. "She's doing it again."

"She's doing what she did to us? What she did to you?"

Another sigh. "Yeah."

"Oh, Jan," she said, shocked and sad at once.

"Yeah," he said again, and paused. Then he explained about the staff meeting, the video linkup, and what Tandy had said. And then he took a deep breath and said, "I saw the kid, Janis. She's given him some bullshit title – head of global operations or something. Sorry."

"I work with teenagers, remember? I've heard worse. Go on."

"Right." She heard a smile in his voice. "Anyway, FAE is planning to implement a worldwide network of kids with our abilities, and they intend to put one on Mars, too. That's why they're involved with Project Terraform."

She thought about that for a moment. "You said there was a military component to the project," she said. "Will the kids be used as a weapon?"

"That's their cover story, at least," he said. "But there's more to it. Look, I'd rather talk about this in person. How soon can you get away?"

She consulted her mental calendar and shook her head ruefully. "There's no way I can leave early. I'm here 'til 3:30 when school ends, and then there's a meeting I have to attend. The father of one of our seniors is coming in for a conference about a library book his son damaged."

"I'm sorry," he said.

"There's nothing to be sorry for," she said. Then she smiled mischievously. "I'm actually looking forward to this meeting. The father has it coming, and I'm going to give it to him."

"Remind me not to get on your bad side, Mrs. Fowler," he said dryly.

"I will," she returned. "Anyway, it isn't your fault your meeting happened on a day when I have to stay late."

She could hear a touch of amusement in his voice. "That's not what I meant, but okay."

"What did you mean, then?" she said, a little more gently.

"I'm sorry you're getting dragged into this all over again. I didn't realize it would affect anyone but me."

"Janusz Marek!" she said. "No one is *dragging* me into anything. I made a choice to see you last week. I could have kicked you out of my library when you opened the door."

"Maybe you should have," he muttered.

"And maybe you shouldn't have gone to that meeting this morning," she said. "Maybe we should never have left the Institute. Or maybe our parents shouldn't have abandoned us there, at the mercy of that woman. There have been thousands of inflection points over the years, and you know as well as I do that no one could have done anything any differently. We would still have ended up here, having this conversation. It was inevitable."

"It *was* inevitable," he agreed.

"It's the only possible result of all the choices made by the people involved."

"Choices have consequences," he said by rote.

"Exactly."

"Dinner, then?"

"Of course." She smiled. "Your place or mine?"

His place was a normal stick-built house, not the Pueblo Revival style of architecture so prevalent in Santa Fe. It was also bigger than her cottage-like casita – three bedrooms instead of just one.

"For a single guy, you bought a lot of house," she observed when he finished showing her around.

He shrugged. "I like the neighborhood. When I first got here, I rented a room from some gay guys who own a house a couple of streets over. It's quiet – nobody looks at you funny if you have an alternative lifestyle." He put air quotes around the phrase.

She cocked her head. "That's the second time you've mentioned being gay. Are you sure you're not in the closet?"

He laughed. "Are you offering to help me figure it out?"

"Are you asking for help?"

He sobered. "I'm not sure."

They gazed at each other for a long moment. "I'm not, either," she admitted. "It's been…"

"…hard."

"…such a long time." She nodded. "And hard. Without you. But being alone feels normal to me now."

"Yeah. Same here." He dropped his gaze, then looked up through his eyelashes at her. She burst out laughing. "What?" he said, chuckling.

"I was just… Oh, God." She braced a hand against the wall and tried to get herself under control. "I just remembered when you used to do that, but you had so much *hair* in the way then."

He ran a hand over his forehead where his unruly bangs used to be. "Way to hurt the old guy's ego," he groused, which set her off again. Which set him off again.

Eyes shining, she said, "You know I wouldn't care if you were bald, right? You'd still be you."

He put his hand on the wall next to her. "I do. I do know." His voice low and husky, he added, "And you're still you."

There was another awkward pause. The kitchen timer broke it. "Thank goodness," he said. "I'm starving."

They made small talk over dinner. Once they were settled near each other on the sofa, he began to expand on what had happened to him earlier in the day.

"It was the oddest experience," he said. "I don't think it's ever happened to me before – meeting someone on another plane of existence, that is."

"What do you mean, another plane of existence?" she asked. "I thought you saw the kid during the videoconference."

"I did. But for a minute at the start of his talk, it was happening somewhere else. The conference room looked the same and everybody attending the meeting looked the same. But everyone in the room had turned to look at me, trying to figure out who the kid was staring at."

"He was in the room with you?"

"No – he was on screen."

"So he was somewhere in Silicon Valley. But you're saying he connected with you through the video link?"

He shrugged. "It's possible. The link goes both ways – we could see everyone in our other offices and they could see us, as well. And hear us, if the mics were turned on everywhere."

"Okay. But he zeroed in on you."

"Right."

She considered that. "Remote viewing, maybe?"

He looked thoughtful. "I suppose it could have been. You and I didn't do much work with remote viewing."

She snorted, remembering her attempts at telesthesia, all of which had ended in abject failure. "Not a talent either of us had."

He smiled crookedly. "True. Although at least my scores were at the level of random chance. Somehow yours were worse."

"That's me," she said cheerfully. "Ask me what you're thinking of, and I'll be wrong ninety-eight percent of the time. But I'm really good at telling you how you felt a week ago last Thursday."

He grinned. "I know."

She circled back to the incident at the meeting. "So the kid – what's his name again?"

"Antoine Jenkins."

"Thank you. So Jenkins contacted you somehow in this other reality. Did he just stare you down, or …?"

"No. He spoke to me."

"And he said…"

"Just one word. 'You.'" He mimicked the young man's intonation as accurately as he could.

Her eyes widened. "It almost sounds like he knew who you were."

"I've been thinking about that. I don't think he did." He turned toward her. "It was more like he was looking for people with talent and happened to find me. That was the sense I got, anyway. It may be the way he does business generally."

"That makes sense. Especially if they're recruiting. And they're going to need a whole lot of folks with abilities similar to ours if they're going to circle the globe."

"There was more to it."

"More than just the contact?"

"Right. I'm pretty sure I didn't open that door. I think he triggered it."

"Triggered…" She reached for his hand. "Oh, Jan."

"Not…" he began, and stopped. He gripped her fingers. "Like I said, I don't think he was after me specifically. I think he was casting a wide net and I happened to get caught. But part of his search process…" He paused again.

She jumped in to try to help. "I think I get where you're going. People with talents like ours have a rough time in life. Society doesn't like

64

weirdness in general, and it's *really* skeptical of paranormal ability. There have been too many charlatans, as well as too many religious leaders who are quick to blame the devil for things that happen out of the ordinary. So a person with these abilities might keep them under wraps to avoid being called crazy.

"I've actually seen that exact thing happen. Some people turn to drugs or alcohol. Some just bury it deep inside. Some do both."

"Your mother," he said.

"She was one, yes. But I've seen it in others."

"Do you know how she's doing?" he asked quietly.

"She's dead," she said matter-of-factly. "Heroin overdose. About twenty years ago. To be honest with you, I was surprised she lived as long as she did."

He covered their joined hands with his other one. He knew better than to say he was sorry for her loss. "Did she ever make it in off the streets?"

"Not really. Sometimes she'd stay clean for a few weeks or months, but she always went back to it. Or so Gigi told me."

"Are you in contact with her?"

She shook her head. "She looked me up when my mother died – to let me know. We emailed back and forth a few times after that, but I haven't heard from her since."

"And Pete?"

She scowled. "Long gone from the picture, and good riddance. Gigi caught him *playing*" – she sketched air quotes around the word – "with a girl in the neighborhood and threw him out. I think that's when she finally acknowledged that my mother hadn't lied to her." She shook her head. "What a mess families are."

"No kidding," he said.

She looked up at him. "What about your parents?"

He smiled, his eyes sad. "I have a sister. Claudia."

"Oh? How old is she?"

"Ten years younger than us." He looked at her. "After my parents had packed me off to the Institute, my mother got pregnant again. They cleaned out my old room and gave it to her. She had no idea she had a brother until a few years ago."

"You went looking for her?"

"No – my parents' lawyer tracked me down to let me know they had both died."

"How?"

"Plane crash on takeoff. They were headed for Hawaii." He was quiet for a moment. "Anyway, I went out to L.A. for their funerals and the reading of the will. They split their estate between the two kids but never bothered to tell either of us about the other."

"That's so bizarre," she said.

He shrugged. "Who knows what went on in my father's head? And Mom just followed his lead."

He sounded so bitter. "I'm sorry about them, anyway. And I'm sorry for your loss."

He glanced at her and looked away.

"So this Claudia," she said. "What's she like?"

"I only met her twice – first at the viewing and then in the lawyer's office. She looks a lot like Mom. *That* was unsettling." He let out a breath. "She has a couple of divorces under her belt. Now she's married to a dentist and living in Encino. She has a couple of grown kids who are turning out grandkids for her." He shrugged. "You know. The usual."

"Right," she said softly. All the usual things the two of them could have had. Should have had. If not for... A sudden fear clutched her heart.

She must have gripped his hand harder than she meant to, because he said, "Tandy doesn't know."

"Are you sure?"

"Reasonably sure. Janis, listen to me." He leaned closer. "Jenkins is a recruiter, not a channel. I didn't feel her lurking in the background. I admit that seeing her scared the shit out of me, but there was absolutely no psychic connection with her. None."

She wanted to believe him, but if Antoine Jenkins had triggered Jan, he had triggered her, too. Was this kid powerful enough on his own to do that?

She shook her head. "I don't know enough about how this stuff works."

"What do you mean?"

"I felt your door open, Jan. Mine opened, too. Right?"

"That's what you said. So?"

"How does his recruiting work? Presumably now that he's tagged you, he can find you. And he's tagged me, too, whether he knows it yet or not." Her heart began thudding harder. "Who does he give his list of prospects to? Who does the legwork to track down their prospects? Does Tandy ever get hold of it?"

"Shh," he said, slipping an arm around her shoulders and pulling her close. "Stop it. You're scaring yourself."

She laid her head on his shoulder, grateful for the contact. "We need to think about this, though. Jenkins may not know who we are, but Tandy will." She freed a hand and put that arm around his waist. "I want you to be safe."

"I'll be fine," he said. *Fine* wasn't the same thing as *safe*, but she let it pass for now. "Hey," he said into her hair. "I didn't tell you what I said to him."

Surprised, she lifted her head to look into his eyes. "You talked to him?"

"I did say the link was two-way."

"So what did you tell him?"

He touched her head and gently guided it back to his shoulder. "I wished him luck. Told him he was going to need it."

She snorted softly. "You didn't."

67

"I did." He rested his cheek against the bun on top of her head. "I meant to wish him good luck getting out of Tandy's clutches, of course."

"Of course."

"It had nothing whatsoever to do with us stopping them, of course."

"Of course not. You would never."

"That's exactly right." He sighed contentedly. "This is nice."

"It is," she agreed. "We should do this more often."

"I intend to," he said.

She smiled and snuggled closer. "Good."

Silicon Valley

Chapter 11

"Curious," Antoine said.

Dr. Tandy – *Denise*, he reminded himself, *she wants me to call her Denise* – continued drawing circles with a fingertip on his bare chest. "Hmm?" she said.

"Oh, nothing."

She sat up and faced him. "It didn't sound like nothing. Tell me."

He tried to focus on her eyes. The rest of her body was a roadmap of scars from all the plastic surgery she had had over the years. When the lights were out, it didn't bother him to fuck a woman who was past eighty. In fact, she was almost obscenely spry for her age. But it wasn't dark now.

"I was just thinking about the meeting with Jemez Aerospace this morning. Kind of going over it in my head."

She raised an eyebrow. "Thinking about work when you should be focusing on me."

Fear shot through him. She had given him so much – all the training to improve his abilities, and the position in her company, and now this … whatever it was. Relationship. Hot granny sex. He couldn't call it friends with benefits – they weren't friends.

His emotions must have been written all over his face. She smirked. "I was joking, Antoine! God, you're so serious all the time." She poked him in the ribs.

He laughed reflexively and flinched away. "Don't. I told you I don't like that."

"That's why I do it." She was still smirking. "But come on – tell me what you were thinking. What's so curious?"

She hadn't poked him again, at least. He relaxed. "It really *was* nothing. I was just thinking about the survey I did before I started to speak."

"You were magnificent, by the way," she said dreamily, drawing lazy circles on his abs again.

"Thanks," he said, grateful as always for her regard.

She watched him through slitted eyes. "What about the survey?"

"Well, the good news is that I discovered three people with sensitivities," he said. "Simone helped me track down two of them. But the third one seems to have evaporated."

"Really."

"Yeah. Weird. First time that's happened to me."

"Maybe it was a false positive," she suggested. "Or some kind of talent echo."

He stroked her upper arm. The tops of her arms weren't too bad, although her skin was crepey. But the undersides were a mass of scar tissue. "I don't think so," he said. "I got something back from him while the meeting was going on. But now he seems to have gone to ground."

"Curious," she said, and covered his mouth with hers.

California, 1974

Chapter 12

"What's this for, anyway?" Janis asked crossly from her seat on the floor. Since she'd turned sixteen, she had gotten into the habit of pulling loose the sofa cushions and using them for floor pillows. Jan didn't understand the attraction, but he often sat on the floor, too, to be closer to her. Plus it was easier to hide from the security camera down here.

Tandy sat primly on the upholstered chair next to the sofa. "Just fill it out, Janis," she said tartly.

"Why should I?"

"Because I asked you to," Tandy said evenly.

Jan caught Tandy's eye and shrugged. He didn't know why Janis was making a big deal about it – it was just a questionnaire, one of about a million Tandy had been giving them in the past year or so. Usually the questions concerned their reactions to the most recent testing they'd been undergoing – whether the exercises had jarred loose any odd dreams or unusual powers they hadn't experienced before – but this new one was a little more personal.

"But you already know about my periods," Janis said. "You've known since I first started having them. You've made me see the doctor a hundred times. Those nasty stirrups – ugh." She made a face. "And no doubt you've seen their reports. What else do you need to know?"

Jan's eyes widened. Nobody had scheduled any doctor appointments for *him*, other than the physical he got every year. And – stirrups? Like on a saddle?

"What I need to know," Tandy went on relentlessly, "are the answers to the questions on that form."

"And what if I refuse?"

Jan had never seen such a wicked grin as Tandy gave Janis just then. "You'll be very sorry."

Janis glared at her.

"Fine," Tandy said, standing up from the chair. "I'll expect to receive the completed form first thing tomorrow morning. You have tonight to fill it out – and to consider what the repercussions might be for disobeying me." She turned to go, and then stopped. "Remember," she said over her shoulder, "choices have consequences." Back straight and head held high, she made her regal departure.

Janis crumpled up her questionnaire and threw both it and her pencil after Tandy. Then she slumped back against the sofa, glowering.

Jan meant to say something calming and placating. But when he opened his mouth, he blurted, "Stirrups?"

"They're these awful things you have to put your feet into," she said. "The doctor makes you take off your bottoms and scoot way down to the end of the exam table. Then you put your feet in the stirrups and he shoves a freezing cold *thing* inside you and feels you all around inside. He plays with your boobs, too. I hate it."

This was all news to Jan. "Nobody's ever played with *my* boobs," he said.

She rolled her eyes. "That's because you don't *have* any." She crossed her arms and leaned back against the front edge of the sofa. "I'm not giving her any more information. I have a right to my privacy!"

Jan glanced down at his own questionnaire. It had some pretty personal questions, too – about hair growth and wet dreams – but it wasn't the first time he'd seen them on one of Tandy's surveys. What had set Janis off?

He got up on his knees and stretched out to retrieve her crumpled form, glancing at her as he did so. He half expected her to tell him to leave it alone, but she didn't – she just watched him while she continued to fume silently. He sat back down and smoothed out the form, then compared her questions to his.

They were different, all right. Tandy wanted to know whether Janis had had sex with him.

76

He stared at the two forms in confusion for a minute or so. Then, slowly, he raised his head. "She never asked *me*," he said.

"I figured," she said. "Since you weren't complaining."

"Right." He passed his questionnaire to her. "I've gotten these same questions two or three times over the past year, maybe. But nothing as invasive as yours."

She read over his form and nodded. "Yeah, see, this is about the level of detail she's wanted from me for the past couple of years. Ever since..." She glanced at him and looked away. "Ever since the day I kissed you."

"I guess that makes sense," he said, although suddenly he felt very warm.

"It does?"

"Sure. Sexual awakening in young teens, and all that junk." He pushed his bangs up out of his face.

"But why does she care?" Janis exploded. "What difference does it make?"

"Maybe she's tracking the effects of puberty on our talents," he guessed. "Whether they mature the same way our bodies do." He was grateful for his bangs slipping back down when he dropped his gaze. "And whether losing your virginity makes a difference."

"But I haven't," she said forcefully.

"Neither have I," he said.

"But she's not asking *you*. She's only asking *me*."

He shrugged again and handed back her wrinkled form. "I have no idea what she's up to. Maybe she'll ask me next week."

That kiss had been their first and last. Not that it hadn't occurred to Jan to try it again. He'd had no objection when it had happened, and the image – and the feelings associated with it – sometimes cropped up in his more explicit daydreams.

But the situation was awkward. He'd grown up with Janis; she was the sister he'd never had. And it seemed kind of wrong to think about having sex with your sister. Kind of gross, really.

Although they weren't siblings.

But she was all the family he had. What would happen if they started something and it didn't work out? What if they ended up hating each other? What if it made it harder for them to have conversations like the one they were having right now?

He noticed her watching him. "I know," she said, as if she'd read his mind. She had uncrossed her arms. Now she sat forward with her forearms on her knees.

He cleared his throat. "I wonder sometimes what it would be like."

"You do?"

"Yeah. Don't you?"

"Of course. All the time."

Without thinking about it, he scooted closer and put an arm around her shoulders. Her head fit perfectly in the space between his shoulder and cheek. She sighed and slipped both arms around his waist.

"What a mess," she said.

"Yeah."

"Maybe we should do it, just to fuck with Tandy."

He chuckled. "I wonder what her reaction would be."

"We could find out easily enough. I could lie on the form."

He found himself grinning. "You wouldn't."

"I might. I need to sleep on it." She snuggled closer. "This is nice."

"It is," he agreed.

A few minutes later, he realized she had fallen asleep. He kissed her hair softly and whispered the words he would never dream of saying when she was awake: "I love you."

Chapter 13

Janis awoke early the next morning, well before her alarm went off. She was tucked in her own bed with her clothes on but her shoes off, and without a memory of how she'd gotten there.

She groaned and sat up. The last thing she remembered was cuddling with Jan on the floor of the lounge. She must have fallen asleep, and he must have gotten her to bed without her waking up enough to remember it.

He'd put her to bed but left her clothes on. What a knight in shining armor.

She yawned and stretched, then threw back the covers and headed for the bathroom. When she came out, she realized her knight hadn't forgotten a thing: he had laid Tandy's crumpled questionnaire in the middle of the top of her otherwise pristine desk. Well, she had plenty of time this morning to fill it out before Tandy got to her office.

She ducked back into the bathroom to take a shower. Maybe the hot water would help her think of what to say.

Forty-five minutes later, she was dressed in clean clothes – jeans and a bright red top – and was regarding the offensive questionnaire. She chewed on her pencil for a moment. Then, rapidly, she began answering Tandy's questions with whatever came to mind. When she got to the question about how far she and Jan had gone sexually, she waffled for a second. But then she rapidly put down her first reaction upon seeing it on the questionnaire the night before:

None of your fucking business, you filthy voyeur.

Satisfied, she used her desktop printer to make a copy for her own file – a practice she had begun with the first too-personal questionnaire a couple of years before. She didn't know what had prompted her to do it, but something told her that file could end up being useful someday. It wasn't her Sight that had prompted her – her talent lay in reading other people's pasts, not in predicting the future – but just a gut feeling that something about this wasn't right, and it might be good to have proof to someday hand to someone who could do something about it.

Janis was suspicious by nature – much more so than Jan. He thought it was because she hadn't bonded properly with her mother, and maybe that was true. All she knew was there weren't many people she fully trusted.

Actually, there was only one person she fully trusted. Jan.

Her copy of the form put away with the others, in a box on the top shelf of her closet, she took the original out of their living quarters and down the hall to Tandy's office.

"Damn," she whispered when she got close. The door was open and light spilled out into the hallway.

She did *not* want to be there when Tandy read her questionnaire. Maybe she could hand it to her and leave. Or put it on the floor just inside the doorway. Or maybe make it into a paper airplane and sail it in. The paper was already wrinkled – she could hardly damage it more.

The thought made her smile – and gave her courage. She was just about to march in and drop her bomb, right in the middle of Tandy's desk, when she heard voices. Well, noises. Grunts and panting.

She stopped one doorway short and listened. It didn't take long.

Tandy's laugh was low and throaty. "You were ready, weren't you?"

"Oh, so ready," came the reply. "I'm always ready for you, Denny."

"And I'm the best lay you've ever had. Right?"

"Nobody's better."

Ick. Janis wrinkled her nose.

The man cleared his throat. "Well. We should get down to business."

"I thought we just did."

"*Before* the rest of the staff arrives."

80

"Oh, all right," Tandy said with a sigh. "You're so tiresome sometimes, Ray."

Janis's eyes widened. Raymond Carruthers was Tandy's boss. She had seen him occasionally in the glass booth with Tandy, listening in one of her training sessions. She was also pretty sure he was married.

It occurred to her that she had never had any insights about Tandy's past. After the first day she had arrived at the Institute, when she Saw that Tandy's mother had never loved her, she had never again been able to get a read on her. Her Sight had kicked in for just about everyone else, from the recording techs to the cleaning crew – but never for Tandy. She wondered if the doctor knew a way to block people with talents from prying into her secrets – and if so, how to do it.

"So what boring subject do we need to discuss this morning?" Tandy said.

"The annual investors' reception," Ray replied.

"The annual shakedown, you mean," she said. "The annual dog-and-pony show."

"It's what keeps us afloat. People will pay anything for information that will help them get a leg up on their competition."

"Yes, I know," she said dismissively. "The receptions were my idea, remember?"

"Of course I remember."

"The economy was bad and contributions were starting to dry up. And I told you we needed to convince our investors they were parting with their cash for a noble cause, wink wink. And it worked. We've had one every year ever since, and we've always netted a big profit. Even without a cash bar."

"Even without the cash bar, yes," Ray replied. It sounded like she'd needled him about it before.

"So what's the issue?" Tandy asked. "I'll get the guest list updated next week and we'll get the invitations in the mail. And I'll have

Accounting pull the catering contract from last year so I can try to negotiate a better deal."

"There's something else," he said.

"You want to freshen up the menu? I hated the Vienna sausages last year. They weren't classy enough for our crowd."

"Denise," he said.

"What?"

"The problem isn't the party. It's our investors."

She paused. "Oh?"

"I've had a few calls over the past couple of months," he said. "People are getting antsy. We've been in operation for almost fifteen years and we've yet to turn a profit."

"I don't understand. We told them all at the start that it would be a long game."

"And getting longer. Look, Denny, you know as well as I do that the economy is souring again. People are taking a hard look at their portfolios. They just want to know when they can begin to expect a return on their investment."

"Well, it will have to be soon, won't it?" she replied in the icy tone she always used with Janis and Jan. "They're sixteen now. Once they turn eighteen, they can legally walk away."

Janis filed that bit of information away to chew over later.

"So sometime in the next year or two?" Ray said. "I'm not sure that answer will be good enough for some of these people."

Both of them were quiet for a moment. Then Tandy said, "Leave it to me. I think I can come up with a way to string them along for another year or two."

"I will leave it in your capable hands, then," Ray said. "Oh. One more thing."

"Yes?" Tandy drew out the word.

"How's your side project coming?"

82

Tandy sighed dramatically. "You know, Ray, I begin to think we made a mistake in the beginning. Maybe we should have segregated them. Isolated them. Made them both yearn for human contact."

Ray sounded amused. "What difference would that make?"

"Maybe they'd see each other as forbidden fruit or something."

"You said they went through puberty on schedule. Do they hate each other?"

"No, not at all. If anything, they're *too* close. Like brother and sister." She let out an explosive sigh. "We're not going to be able to get what we need from them unless they're sexually attracted to each other."

"Denny, I know that's your pet theory," he said. "But what if sex isn't necessary for them to become bound to one another?"

"I've *told* you, Ray," she said, exasperated. "Physical union is the key to unlocking their full potential. Without it, they won't be the weapon we need."

"Well, all right," said Ray, sounding dubious. "Keep me posted."

"I will."

"I could use some coffee," he said, sounding more relaxed. "Somebody dragged me out of bed too early this morning."

"I guess that means I'm paying," Tandy said, a teasing note in her voice.

Janis slipped a hand behind her back, found a doorknob, and turned it. Luck was with her – the door opened. She just had time to slip inside before Ray and Tandy left her office and walked down the hall in the opposite direction.

When she could no longer hear their voices, she breathed an audible sigh of relief. Then she let herself back out, placed her completed questionnaire squarely in the middle of Tandy's desk, and made her way back to their quarters.

She couldn't wait to see Jan. They had so much to discuss.

Chapter 14

Jan's cereal floated in his bowl, the pieces bloated with milk. He wasn't planning to eat any more of it, anyway. The few bites he'd swallowed before Janis burst in with her news were sitting none too comfortably in his stomach.

"So we're supposed to be a weapon?" he said.

"That's what Tandy said. And oh my God, Jan – they're screwing each other! Isn't that crazy?"

Leave it to Janis to focus on Tandy's sex life. "People do, you know," he said. "Screw each other, I mean."

"Yes, of course," she said impatiently. "I had the same sex ed course you did." She paused. "I think I did, anyway. You did cover the mechanics of how humans reproduce, right? Not just the G-rated version?"

He rolled his eyes. "Yes, of course. Penis meets vagina and so on. Could we maybe focus on the part where we're supposed to be a weapon?"

She shrugged. "That's honestly all I know. Ray said the investors are getting nervous because they haven't made any money yet." She frowned. "But Tandy said they were told originally that their contributions were going toward a noble cause. Although she sounded sarcastic when she said it."

"So they lied to these people," Jan said. "Or else everybody's in on the con. The 'noble cause' story is the cover for the real operation."

"Us," Janis said.

"Right. Us. And how do we get to be a weapon?"

Her eyes met his. "We bond through intercourse, apparently."

He let out a sigh and shook his head. "How can you manage to say that so matter-of-factly?"

"Because it's what she *said*, Jan. Honestly, you're such a weenie about this stuff sometimes. Are you done with your cereal?" She stood and put a hand out for his bowl.

He handed it over. "It's not that I find the idea distasteful," he began.

"You're doing wonders for my confidence," she threw at him, and headed for the kitchen.

He followed her. "You know that's not what I meant." He folded his arms and leaned a shoulder against the door jamb, filling the space. He had shot up over the past few months, and his shoulders had broadened.

She dumped their uneaten food down the chute and put the bowls and spoons in the sink for the cleaners. Then she turned to him, glaring. "Move. I need to get to class."

"Not yet," he said. "Listen to me. What sort of weapon are they trying to make us into? And do we want to help them get what they want?"

She looked away. "I don't know." When he didn't say anything, she looked back at him. "I don't *know*, Jan. I don't know *what* to think."

"Neither do I. And I think that's by design. They've kept us in the dark about everything. We've been isolated from our families, our friends, everyone except the people on staff here. They pick the books we read and the TV programs we watch. They control everything we can learn about the world outside of this place. And it's been going on for *years*."

"You make it sound like we're in prison," she said in a small voice.

"Aren't we?"

She stared at him for a moment. "I've got to get to class," she said again, and tried to push past him. His arm shot out to stop her, and suddenly he was kissing her.

Just as suddenly, she pushed away from him and ran for her room.

He wiped his mouth with the back of one hand. Then he fled to his own room.

Both of them were late to class. The tutor eyed them impatiently as they took their seats, then launched into an intricate discussion of some important law of physics.

He seemed to think it was important, anyway. Janis had trouble concentrating and could not answer a single question correctly.

At the end of class, she beat Jan out the door – and found Tandy waiting for her in the hallway. "Janis. In my office, if you please," she said. "Now." She turned on her heel and walked away.

"This day just keeps getting better and better," she muttered as she followed dutifully.

Tandy allowed her to go in first and gestured to the guest chair nearest the door. Janis wondered whether Ray had sat there that morning. Then she wondered where they'd done the deed. On the couch along the wall? On her desk? A mental picture formed of Tandy on her back amid the clutter on her desk, with Ray looming over her…

Ick. She resolutely pushed it away.

Tandy sat in her own chair. She folded her hands and put her forearms on the desk between them. "I read your responses," she said.

Janis waited, trying not to be too obvious about how hard she was clutching the arms of the chair.

"I am sorry you did not see the need to take this more seriously," Tandy went on, once it was clear Janis wasn't going to respond. "The Institute has done so much for you. So *very* much for you. We have fed you and clothed you. Educated you. Helped you to develop your talent in interesting and intriguing ways." She paused. "You were so small when you arrived. So trusting. Sometimes I feel like I've raised you." She chuckled.

I wasn't as trusting as you think.

"And we've asked so little from you in return," Tandy went on. "We expect you to do well in your classes and in your abilities tests. And we expect you to *cooperate.*"

Still, Janis was silent.

"What would happen to you if we turned you out?" Tandy asked. "Hmm? Where would you go? Who would help you?"

No one. No one would help me. I have nowhere to go. No one to trust.

Tandy must have seen her barbs hit home, because she smiled. "I'm glad we understand one another now." She passed Janis a piece of paper. "Here is a clean copy of the questionnaire. Please complete it – *honestly* this time – and have it back to me by the end of the day."

She couldn't hold it in any longer. "But why on earth do you need to know whether Jan and I have slept together?"

In response, Tandy simply smiled.

Janis snatched up the paper. At the door, she turned and shot a barb of her own. "Tell me, Dr. Tandy. Does Mr. Carruthers' wife know why he had to be at work so early this morning?" She took satisfaction in watching the play of emotions on Tandy's face: shock, then anger. Maybe even hatred. With a victorious smile, she turned and walked out.

Safely back in her own room, she sat down at her desk and took slow, deliberate breaths – in, out. In, out. Then she took up her pencil and filled out the form. For the nasty question, she wrote the truth:

No.

She made a copy and filed it, and walked the original back to Tandy.

The doctor was writing something on a pad of paper when she walked in. Janis held out the form. Tandy took it without looking up.

Then Janis went back to their quarters, left a note for Jan saying she wasn't feeling well, and went to bed. Maybe, she thought, the day will be better after a reset.

Jan found the note she had taped to the door of his room and wondered what had made her feel sick. Was it something Tandy had said to her after physics class? Or was it left over from breakfast, when he'd shat all over her news and told her maybe they shouldn't be together, and then kissed her? Talk about mixed messages. Jan Marek, lady killer.

To tell the truth, he wasn't feeling all that well himself. Maybe he'd skip class this afternoon, too.

He realized immediately what a bad idea that was. One of them had to show up or Tandy would come looking for them both. It had happened before, when they were much younger. Tandy called it playing hooky, and they'd ended up with double the homework.

He wrote at the bottom of Janis's note:

Sorry you feel sick. I hope you feel better soon. I'll take notes for both of us.
See you tonight.

He really did hope she would feel better, and not only because she was his friend. He hoped her afternoon off would help her find some better answers to their situation.

After class, he was scheduled to work with Tandy on his future envisioning skills, so he headed to the training room.

He wasn't excited about going, partly because these sessions were becoming increasingly pointless. Tandy constantly asked him to do stuff that was outside his skill set, and every time she insisted he try again, it made him feel like more of a failure. Lately, she had seemed disappointed in his lack of progress, and that made him feel worse. It wasn't that he yearned for her approval or anything, but her disappointment seemed to dredge up the feelings he had when he was a kid – when his parents seemed to want him to be perfect and he knew he never would be.

His ego was already taking a beating over his mixed-up feelings for Janis. The last thing he needed was to have someone else point out how less-than-perfect he was.

What he really wanted to do was go back to their quarters. He was anxious to find out how Janis was feeling, and he also wanted to let her know that she hadn't missed anything in class. The tutor didn't feel

88

comfortable discussing the reading assignment without her, so he gave Jan the period to read whatever he wanted.

That's what he told himself his motivation was, anyway.

His thoughts awhirl, he pushed open the training room door and settled his books in their accustomed cubby near the door. It was only then, when he turned around to go to his seat, that he realized he wasn't alone. Tandy stood across the room, an odd look on her face.

"Aren't we doing training today?" he asked, glancing toward the glass-enclosed booth where she usually sat with the recording tech.

"Ron had an errand to run," she said. "He'll be here in a little while." She moved closer, blocking his route to his seat. "I thought we could take this opportunity to talk."

This was brand-new. "Okay," Jan said, on his guard. "What do you want to talk about?"

She walked to a spot just behind his seat and ran her fingers across the back. "I know I've been a little hard on you over the last few weeks. I can see how it's beginning to affect your performance."

Jan didn't know what to say, so he didn't say anything.

"You have to understand," she said, still trailing her fingers across the chair back, "I'm not trying to be cruel. I do these things for a reason." She gave him a sidelong glance and a coy smile. "You do understand that, don't you?"

"Uh, sure," he said. "I'm sure there are a lot of things you haven't told us about."

Her fingers stilled for a moment, then resumed their slow back-and-forth motion. It occurred to him that she was almost caressing the chair. "Yes," she said. "There are. Lots of things I haven't told you. Because I'm an adult."

"Because you run the program," he said slowly.

She ignored that. "What I'm trying to say is ... you're a very attractive young man, Jan. And sometimes it's hard for me to remember that I'm the adult and you're still a child." She looked up at him then. "Do you understand what I'm saying?"

"Kind of," he said.

She moved toward him. "I know all about you, you know," she said. "Everything you think about. All your feelings. How you've … matured." She was close enough now to touch him. She rested one hand lightly on his shoulder and began moving her fingers back and forth, back and forth.

His body reacted to her touch in ways he'd never experienced before, and it made him profoundly uncomfortable. He took a short step back. "Look, maybe I should come back once Ron gets here."

She stepped forward, closing the gap between them. "Tell me, Jan," she said, her voice low, "do you ever think about me?"

Her hips twitched against him. He could hardly avoid thinking about her right now. He swallowed hard.

She twined both of her arms around his neck. "I could make you a man," she said, breathing in his ear. "Would you like that?"

"I have to go," he said. He pulled her arms down and escaped without even stopping to grab his books from the cubby.

He dearly hoped he could make it to his room without running into anyone. He needed a cold shower to get his physical response to Tandy under control. But of course Janis was lounging on the floor, and he couldn't just run past her without saying anything.

"You're better," he said, wishing he had something to hold in front of his crotch.

"Yeah, I took a nap." She peered at his face. "What happened to you?"

"Nothing! I have to go." He started for his room.

She intercepted him. "Don't give me that. What happened?" Her brow lowered. "It was Tandy, wasn't it?"

His shoulders slumped. He should have known Janis wouldn't let him off the hook. "Yeah. She made a pass at me."

"What? Oh, Jan." Her hand rested on his shoulder – right where Tandy had …

"Don't *do* that!" He jerked away.

She pulled her hand away as if he'd burned her. "I'm sorry! I didn't …"

He went on to his room and opened the door. She was right behind him. "What on earth has gotten into you?" she cried, exasperated. "Jan! Talk to me!" She grabbed his hand and spun him around.

He groaned and pulled her into his arms. Then he kicked the door shut. He made sure she was close – closer than Tandy had been. And without another word, his mouth came down on hers, hard.

He was half out of his mind, but part of his brain was still functioning. He kind of expected her to push him away, as she had that morning. Maybe even slap his face.

But no. She melted into the kiss. His tongue found its way into her mouth and she seemed to like it there. In the meantime, his hands were busy, traveling to her butt, molding her to him.

She gasped and began to pull his shirt out of his pants. That seemed like a good idea, so he began to untuck her blouse. His hands traveled up her back and around to her breasts.

In another minute, both of them were on the bed and shirtless. He wasn't quite sure how it had happened – only that it gave him a better look at her breasts. Her bra needed to go, he was sure, and soon it was gone.

When her hand unzipped his jeans and touched his penis through the fabric of his underwear, the world exploded.

She laughed in delight, and he laughed too. "Your turn," he said, and slid his hand beneath her panties. Soon she cried out, and then joined him in happy laughter.

A little while later, he said, "I wonder if we're joined now."

"I think technically we're still virgins," she said.

"So we can keep doing this?" he asked. "And not play into their scheme?"

"I hope so," she said.

"So do I," he said. "So do I."

New Mexico

Chapter 15

Janis made it a practice to stay far away from the school building on weekends. The HVAC system was either turned off or set so low, or so high, that working in the building for any length of time was uncomfortable. Teachers who worked with the kids on extracurricular activities could put in a request to have it turned on, but Janis had never done any of that.

Still, as an educational facility, the school library had research resources she couldn't tap at home. So she braced herself for a sweltering June Saturday and headed in to work.

Somebody must have had something going on that day, because the library was comfortably temperature-controlled. She hoped it was a good omen for what she was about to do.

She left her lunch bag and purse in her office and closed the door. Then she took a seat at the information desk and logged in. And then she began looking for dirt on the internet for the Foundation for the Advancement of Excellence.

She decided the Wikipedia entry must have been written by the FAE's public relations department. There was very little about the organization's history but a whole lot of bland prose that didn't say much of anything. She clicked through to the FAE website and had her suspicions confirmed; the Wikipedia article had been lifted, nearly word for word, from the front page of the site. The mission statement was equally murky.

Next, she tried the "who we are" link. There, she found a short biography of Tandy, complete with an old photo. Janis had done the math – the woman had to be over eighty, yet she looked to be in her mid-forties here. The deception didn't really surprise Janis. As a middle-aged woman herself, she knew first-hand how society viewed them: Once you got past the ingenue stage, if you didn't keep your looks up, you might as well not exist. It wasn't right and it wasn't fair, but it was reality.

"When I'm queen," Janis said in a little singsong, "things will be different." Her lips curled in a sly smile. *Things will be different soon. And I know someone who will never be queen, if Jan and I can help it.*

She turned to the biography and snorted. Dr. Tandy, it said, had devoted her life to helping children reach their full potential. "Of course she doesn't say *how*," she muttered. She noted the reference to "decades of experience" but no mention of the Institute. Not that she had expected to find one. But it was a little disheartening to find no mention at all of the place where she and Jan had grown up – even though that was exactly what they'd been after. If the Institute had ruined their lives, the least they could do was ruin the Institute.

She scrolled down the page and got her first look at the young man Jan always called "the kid." Antoine Jenkins looked almost joyous in his photo. His biography was awfully thin for someone who was purportedly vice president of a global corporation: Supposedly he'd earned an M.B.A., but the school was not one she'd ever heard of. She made a note to try to find it. Regardless, all of his experience appeared to be with FAE, and that didn't surprise Janis at all.

She scrolled down to review the rest of the C-suite and bumped against the bottom of the page. There were no other officers listed – just Tandy and this Antoine. Who at NASA had vetted them for the contract? For all anybody knew, they could be the only two employees.

FAE had a board of directors, though, apparently. She clicked that link and spotted more familiar names – among them, Raymond Carruthers, who had been Tandy's boss once upon a time. Janis wondered idly whether he was still married – and whether he and Tandy were still having an affair. He had to be pushing ninety by now.

She recognized many of the other board members from the Institute's fundraising receptions – and she realized now that they had all been politicians and corporate bigwigs. She and Jan hadn't thought much about them. All the two of them knew was they had money, and Tandy wanted as much of it as she could get her hands on in order to keep her sketchy business afloat.

A couple of the names were new since her involvement with the Institute. She opened a new tab and looked them up. It turned out one of them was with NASA. "I guess that's how they got the contract," she said aloud. "Quid pro quo. A seat on the board for an in on the Mars mission."

The address on the contact page of the website also rang a bell. FAE was working out of the same facility that had housed the Institute, back in the day. She looked it up on Google Maps but could only get as far as the front gate – the driveways inside weren't mapped. Even the satellite photo appeared to be pixelated.

She looked up Antoine's alma mater and found nothing but a link back to its mention in his FAE bio. It looked as though she had been right – the school didn't exist.

On a whim, she ran a search on Tandy herself – and there, at last, she found something enlightening. About ten years before, the doctor had been interviewed by an investment guru for his podcast. Janis had no interest in listening to the audio – she'd had enough of Tandy's voice to last her a lifetime and then some – but somebody on the guru's staff had transcribed the show. She sent the transcript and the bios from the FAE website to the printer. And she collected one other thing from FAE's site – an annual report. She figured it wouldn't be any more enlightening than the brochures the Institute's would-be investors were given back in the day, but it might provide her with a lead or two on where to search next.

Having thoroughly mined FAE's scanty website, she knocked off for lunch. She ate her sandwich and an apple while looking over what she'd found so far.

A search for the "Institute" would be too broad, she knew; she was likely to get several million hits on schools and nonprofits that had nothing to do with Tandy's operation. She hadn't tried pairing the term with Tandy's name yet, though, so she did. It turned up nothing worthwhile.

But her gut told her to run one last search – this one on Tandy and Carruthers. And there, she found a tantalizing tidbit about what the two of them had been up to during the past forty years. Carruthers had been profiled in his fraternity's magazine, and somehow it had gotten posted on the internet on the public side of the membership paywall.

Not only did the article mention Tandy, but there was also an oblique reference to the Institute. Carruthers, she learned, came from a very wealthy family. He had used his share of the family fortune to buy the land the Institute was built on. He had met Tandy at a conference, and the two of them had envisioned the Institute originally as a place for paranormal research.

How that odd but innocuous-seeming idea had morphed into a virtual prison for two talented kids, the article didn't say.

It did touch on how most people laughed at the idea of extrasensory perception, or ESP, being real. There was a mention of someone named Kreskin and his ability to bend spoons with his mind, which Tandy had never had them try. But Carruthers was convinced ESP and other paranormal phenomena existed. "I've experienced some very unusual things," he was quoted as saying.

"Ghosts?" the interviewer wanted to know.

"No, nothing like that. But mental telepathy is real," Carruthers insisted. "I've had instances where I've had insights into events that I could not have known about any other way. And Denise, my partner in this venture, is also sensitive."

Janis's eyes widened. Tandy was talented? She knew without a doubt that the woman was a sociopath, but *talented*? Then why trap the two of them to mine *their* Sight to make a buck? Why not use her own? It made no sense.

She didn't doubt that Carruthers believed Tandy had a talent similar to hers and Jan's. But she thought it far more likely that Tandy had discovered Carruthers' interest in the paranormal and told him she had a sensitivity to reel him in. She might even have tricked him into believing he had read her mind once or twice.

Carruthers may have been Tandy's first mark.

And now she had Antoine Jenkins on a string. And a whole host of other talented people around the world, if her speech to Jan's company could be believed.

She printed the article about Carruthers, too. Then she packed up her lunch trash and her hard copies, logged out, and got in her car to drive to Jan's.

He was waiting for her. "Anything?" he asked as he let her in his front door.

"Maybe." She gave him a sisterly peck on the cheek and dropped her purse by the door. "It's a hot one out there today."

"I know. I tried to get in a little yardwork, but it was broiling. I hope the monsoons show up on time this year."

She gave him a sidelong smile. "I still cannot get over that we've lived so close to each other for all these years and didn't know it. Nobody outside the Southwest would understand the significance of our summer rains."

He smiled. "It does seem like more than a coincidence."

"I'm sure of it." She smiled back, then handed him her stack of printouts. "Here you go. A little light reading for you."

"Wow." He flipped through them quickly. "I hope they don't charge you by the page."

"The librarian has a budget," she said airily. She had put the article about Carruthers on top. "Read that first."

"Want anything?" he said, heading for the couch.

"Water. I'll get it myself." She walked into the kitchen and availed herself of the in-door icemaker. "I've always wanted one of these," she said over the *plop* of the cubes into her glass. "So bourgeois."

"That's me – bougie to the core."

She grinned, then settled herself on the couch next to him and let him read the article without further interruption.

He had the same reaction she had – disbelief. "Tandy is talented?"

"You never saw any evidence of it, either, huh?"

He shook his head as he flipped back to the paragraph where Carruthers claimed she was sensitive. "No. Never."

"I think she took him for a ride," Janis said.

"Well," said Jan with a sly smile, "we knew about that at the time."

She slapped his shoulder. "You're terrible. No, I mean I think she set him up."

"Plausible." He nodded thoughtfully. "It wouldn't have been hard to do, if he was primed to believe in it to start with."

"Exactly. He was gullible, and she took advantage of him. I think she made him into her meal ticket."

"I think you're right," he said. He looked up at her. "And then the two of us showed up, and it turned out paranormal phenomena were real, after all."

"Just not exactly the way she'd thought," Janis said.

Jan flipped the article over and put it on the coffee table. "What else have you got?"

"Not much." She showed him the bio page from FAE's website. "That's the kid you saw, right?"

"Yep, that's him." Jan studied the photo for a moment. "God, he's young."

"His M.B.A. is from a school that doesn't exist." She pointed to the line in Antoine's bio, using the opportunity to lean against him.

He took the hint and put an arm around her shoulders. "Big surprise about the kid's school," he said. "I see Tandy's bio isn't very detailed."

"Oh – there's an article." She helped him page through the printouts. "Here."

He glanced at the name of the website and did a double-take. "Hey, I've heard of this guy."

"You have?"

"Yeah. He claims to be a wizard at picking solid investments before anyone else. I've listened to a few of his podcasts. Even followed his advice once or twice."

She gazed up at him merrily. "Did you make a killing?"

"I haven't quit my day job, have I?" He arched an eyebrow, then glanced over the transcript. "That's interesting."

"Hmm?"

"Usually his guests are experts of one sort or another – economists or financial analysts. I wonder why he asked her on the show?" He fell silent as they both read it. Janis hadn't taken the time to do more than skim it before.

"Well," Jan said at last, "I can see why he never asked her back. Just being on the show is supposed to be free publicity for your employer, but she couldn't help herself – she had to plug her company at every opportunity."

"Bad form?" she asked.

"Very bad." Then he paused. "You know, I've heard of her company." He got up and fetched a laptop from the breakfast bar. As he settled back in, he gave her a look of chagrin. "I have a bad habit of reading the newspaper online while I eat breakfast."

"Aha! The truth comes out," she said.

"I know. I should be ashamed of myself. You'll know *all* my secrets before this is over." He brought the laptop to life, opened a browser window, and plugged in the name of the company Tandy had kept mentioning on the podcast.

When the results came back, Janis whistled. "No wonder you thought the company sounded familiar. The Justice Department brought fraud charges against them."

"And against a bunch of the corporation's officers, which is pretty unusual. Typically the top people are shielded by a corporate veil so they're protected from any legal action brought against the company. That didn't happen this time."

"Look who they charged," said Janis.

Jan sat back and looked at her, a slow smile spreading over his face. "Raymond Carruthers," he said. "And he was convicted. This explains where he was for part of the past forty years."

"In prison," Janis said. "I wonder where Tandy was during all that time."

"Softening up another mark would be my guess. In case he couldn't get parole."

"But now they're working together again on this FAE project," said Janis. "She must have waited for him. Isn't that sweet?"

"That's one word for it," he said. He shut down the laptop and put it on the coffee table atop the printouts Janis had brought over. "I'm hungry. How about we order pizza?"

"That sounds fine," she said, and they dickered over toppings for a couple of minutes. Then he called in the order.

Janis couldn't help it; her eyes misted over. He noticed when he came back to the couch. "What's this all about?" he asked.

She chuckled and dabbed at her eyes. "It's silly."

"Tell me."

"It's all just so *normal*," she said. "Sitting here with you, like the last forty years never happened. And now someone's going to bring us a *pizza*. On a *Saturday night*." She sighed and wiped at her eyes again. "All these years. All the normal things couples do – we never had a chance to do them."

He pulled her against him. "We have the chance now. And I do not mean to let it slip away."

102

Chapter 16

Not to be outdone, Jan did some snooping of his own on Monday. He'd spent the previous day going over the rest of Janis's hard-copy documents, but there wasn't much more to be gleaned from them. He had hoped for a glimmer of transparency in FAE's annual report, but it was as shrouded in doublespeak as the company's website.

He knew how to get more information on the Mars project, though. And by doing it, he would warm the cockles of his boss's heart. So he presented himself to Dan first thing Monday and spoke the V word.

For a moment, Dan stared at him. "The apocalypse is coming, right? Because I can't think of anything else that would make you volunteer for *any*thing."

The comment about the apocalypse wasn't far off the mark, but Jan wasn't about to tell him that. "I just think it would be an interesting challenge," he said, taking a seat in Dan's guest chair.

"Uh-huh. How many interesting challenges have I offered you that you've turned down flat?"

"But *space travel*, Dan," he said, trying to inject some excitement into his voice. "What kid of the '70s could walk away from that?" He frowned. "Don't tell me you never read science fiction when you were a kid."

"Of course I did. *And* I watched Neil Armstrong play golf on the moon. I totally understand why you'd be excited to be on this team."

Jan *tsk*ed. "Alan Shepard."

"What?"

"It was Alan Shepard who played golf on the moon."

Dan raised an eyebrow at him. "You're sure about that."

"Of course I'm sure. Neil Armstrong and Buzz Aldrin were the first guys to set foot on the moon, but it was Shepard who thought to bring his clubs." As Dan continued to look askance at him, he said, "Look it up if you don't believe me. Your computer's right there." He waved toward the monitor on Dan's desk.

"No, no, that's fine," his boss said. "I don't need to check up on you. If you say it wasn't Neil Armstrong, I believe you."

Jan stifled a grin. "Right."

Dan sighed. "Okay, smart guy, you're on the team. I would have done it sooner if I'd thought you were interested." He shook his head. "I'll have Ed take over Project Tau – that should clear your schedule for Terraform. Bennie Deng's the team leader – you get along with him, don't you?"

Jan assumed an innocent air. "I get along with everybody, boss."

"Mostly," he grumbled. "Anyway, go talk to him. And let me email Ed to tell him I'm dumping your work on him."

Jan grinned and stood. "Thanks, Dan. I mean it. This means the world to me."

"Get out of my office," Dan mock-growled.

Jan paused at the door. "Open or shut?"

"Open is fine." So Jan left it open. He was three feet down the hall when he heard Dan say, "Damn. It *was* Alan Shepard!"

Bennie was a good guy, if not the most loquacious. Part of it was because of the language barrier – Bennie's family had emigrated to America from China when he was in high school, and he still spoke English with an accent that made him hard for the average American to understand. Math, though, he had no trouble with. He had earned a Ph.D. in astrophysics, and that had gotten him the job with Jemez Aerospace.

He waved when Jan entered his office and grunted upon hearing he'd joined the Terraform team. He rose from his desk and stood on tiptoes to reach the top shelf of a tall bookcase, where he had stored several thick binders. He pulled one down and handed to Jan. "Here's the briefing book," he said. "Restricted access. Eyes only." He pointed an index and middle finger at his own eyes.

"Sure, I understand." He began thumbing through it.

"Team meeting tomorrow at eight. Have it memorized by then." He grinned. "Kidding. But take time to look it over before then."

"My schedule is pretty clear this afternoon," he said. "I need to stop by and chat with Ed about Project Tau, but after that I'm all yours."

Bennie flashed him a thumbs up. "Great. We need you."

"You should have come with us last Saturday night," Ed said, as he took a box of Project Tau binders from Jan.

"Oh?"

"Yeah. The place was hopping with women. I think I made a score." Ed grinned, pleased with himself.

"Will wonders never cease," Jan said. "Congratulations. What's her name?"

"I shouldn't tell you. I don't want to jinx anything." But he leaned over his desk and said confidentially, "It's Marnie." He leaned back and resumed a normal tone. "I've seen her there before, but last weekend was the first time I had a chance to chat her up, you know? And she's great. In fact" – he leaned forward again – "she may just be the one."

"Really? That's great, Ed," Jan said. "Congratulations." He put as much surprise and pleasure into his voice as he thought plausible.

"Thanks. So what's new in your life?"

Jan grinned. "Work and more work. I need to get going, in fact. I've got a big binder to get through before the Terraform team meeting tomorrow. I just stopped by to bring you my stuff for Tau."

Ed waved him off. "Go on, then. Enjoy."

"Oh, I will," Jan said. "I'm really looking forward to this project, Ed. It's the opportunity of a lifetime."

Several hours later, Jan sat back and rubbed his face with both hands. The Project Terraform briefing binder was several weeks out of date; it had tons of information about Jan's company's work on the project, but nothing about FAE's plans. He could speculate, based on what he saw here, but nothing more than that. It looked like he would have to wait until the meeting in the morning to learn anything useful. Which was just as well – he was beginning to have trouble focusing on the words on the page, which meant he'd forgotten to take breaks to rest his eyes. His optometrist would have no sympathy for him, either.

"Getting old stinks," he muttered. He tilted his head back and closed his eyes.

All at once, his Sight kicked in.

He had a view of Earth from a thousand miles up. As the globe rotated below him, he noticed white dots blinking here and there across the planet – several in Europe, one in Australia, two in Asia, two in South America, even one in Antarctica. They were connected by a thin tracing of silver – a two-way path, he realized, for exchanging impressions and information. Bigger white dots glowed in North America, with the biggest – the hub – in California.

As he watched the light show, a rocket took off from the New Mexican desert near White Sands. He followed its trajectory skyward and noted when it left Earth's atmosphere. His view expanded, allowing him to track the spacecraft's flight to Mars. The trip happened a whole lot quicker than it would in real time; within seconds, the craft was orbiting Mars and a shuttlecraft left its bay for the trip to the surface.

As it landed, a spaceport grew up around it. Jan saw that those who lived and worked there were both military and civilian personnel – and one of the civilians glowed like the nodes he had seen back on Earth. Gradually, a silver pathway established itself from that pulsing white light to the hub in Silicon Valley.

Then another dot showed up – this one on Earth's moon. And another on one of Jupiter's moons. Those nodes connected themselves

106

in turn to the California hub – but they also joined to send a new silver pathway out into space.

Jan couldn't see the terminus for that pathway, but he sensed it existed. He was certain that if he could find out who or what was at the other end, all of his questions would be answered. So he reached with his Sight, out along this interstellar path, trying to discover where it ended.

A low chuckle sounded in his head. "Found ya," a voice said.

Instantly, Jan slammed down the connection. He recognized that voice. It belonged to the kid – Antoine Jenkins. He had laid a trap for Jan, and Jan had taken the bait. Just a few moments more and the kid would have known who he was.

Jan came back to himself at his desk, soaked in sweat. He ran a trembling hand through his hair and glanced at the time on his computer. Then he took a deep, calming breath. He had been in the trance, or whatever it was, for only a few minutes. The vision had been so vivid – more vivid than any he had ever previously experienced – that he was afraid he had checked out for hours.

Still, it was unnerving. Jenkins had built quite an impressive fantasy world for him to get lost in – and he'd tapped into Jan's Sight to do it. It made Jan's own ability look like a parlor trick.

Moreover, he had always trusted his Sight to show him the future accurately. It might outline several paths, but the end – the terminal event – was always clear. How could he trust his ability if someone could turn it against him? How could he tell what was true?

He got up and paced around his desk to the window. Then he took a seat in his own guest chair. Sometimes the physical change in perspective helped him to see a problem from a different angle – and this was definitely a problem.

From this chair, he could see the road that ran past the office park where he worked. For a few moments, he watched cars going by in both directions.

Both directions.

The link Jenkins had tricked him into establishing went both ways. Maybe he could exploit that.

Silicon Valley

Chapter 17

"Damn!" Antoine said. He sprang up from the sectional sofa and began pacing from one end of the room to the other. It was a huge room – almost like a reception area – with a pantry off one end. His office, complete with full bath, was down the hall.

His assistant, Simone, poked her head around the corner. "Everything okay in there?"

"I almost had him," Antoine said. He held up his hand, thumb and forefinger a tiny bit apart, and shook it. "I was *this close* to nailing the bastard. But he shut me down again. How does he *do* that?" He blew out an exasperated breath and threw himself onto the sectional's long end.

"Maybe he's no prize, after all," she said.

"Oh, no. No, he's *good*. He's the real deal, Mony."

Simone joined him, taking a seat at the short end of the sectional. He marveled anew at how beautiful she was. Her hair was done up today in a side braid with extensions that were almost golden – a striking contrast to her tight black blazer and short pencil skirt that revealed more about her figure than was strictly professional. She was already tall, but her stiletto heels made her taller. And she was smart, too. "What about those other people you were tracking down?"

"Yeah, about them," he said. "None of them panned out. They all had a *little* talent – enough to ping my web – but none of them are strong enough for the long haul. *This* guy, though." He sat up, forearms on his knees. "How does he keep getting away?"

She smoothed her skirt. "Did you get anything on him? A location? His surroundings?"

"A bone to throw Dr. Tandy?" he said, saying the quiet part out loud. "I wish I had. He was in an office, that's all. Normal desk, normal chair. Blank white walls. Very boring."

"Anything on his desk?"

"He never looked at it."

"But did *you* look at it?"

He sighed. "Didn't think of it, to tell you the truth. I was too busy reeling him in. Stupid." He smacked a fist into his other palm in frustration.

"Aww, don't be too hard on yourself," she said. "It sounds like you're making progress. Yesterday you weren't sure you'd ever be able to make contact again, and now you have."

"For a minute." He sat quietly for a moment, his hands fisted in front of his mouth. Then he glanced at her with a small smile. "I know one thing now, though. He's a major space geek. He was ready to follow that filament all the way out into the great beyond."

"You mean he fell for it?"

"The cover story? Yeah. I mean, it looks like he did."

She tilted her head. "So why *are* we getting involved with this Mars mission, anyway?"

"Well, it's not to search for aliens," he said with a snort. Then he got serious. "Sorry, Mony. I really can't tell you. It's all classified and need-to-know."

"It's okay. I get it." She rose to her feet gracefully. "Maybe you'll have better luck tomorrow. You know you have a meeting with the Terraform team first thing, right?"

"Yeah. And of course you're right. Maybe he'll be there and show himself." He leaned back. "Either way, I need to line him up pretty quick. He's our best prospect right now. Hell, he's our *only* prospect right now."

She gave him an encouraging smile. "Well, I predict you'll have a *big* breakthrough tomorrow morning."

"I hope so," he said. "Dr. Tandy wants a report from me by Wednesday. If I can't nail this guy by then, I won't have anything to give her."

"Is that a problem?" Simone asked.

Antoine shuddered. "I don't want to disappoint her. She hates it when I disappoint her."

New Mexico

Chapter 18

"Absolutely not," Janis said. The smothered burrito she'd had for dinner was beginning to turn over unpleasantly in her stomach.

Jan leaned across her dinette table and gripped her forearm. "But this is our best chance," he said. "We *have* to know what FAE is up to. If I can make contact with this kid…"

"And pry into his mind the way he did to you," she said. "You don't *have* that kind of skill, Jan."

"I told you," he said. "I've been thinking about what he does. Going over it in my head. I think I can reverse engineer it."

"And what if it doesn't work?"

"I'll sever the connection, the same way I did this afternoon," he said. "I don't see why you're…" A moment later, his eyebrows shot up and his voice softened. "You're afraid."

"You're damned right I'm afraid," she shot back. "I'm so afraid for you, I feel like I'm gonna puke."

His mouth quirked up at one corner. "Don't do that. It would be a waste of good Mexican food."

"It *was* a superb burrito," she admitted. "But don't change the subject. I'm not going to let you sacrifice yourself."

"The way we both sacrificed ourselves all those years ago?" he said.

"Yes. Exactly." She paused. "Let me do it instead."

He laughed. "Not on your life."

"I'm the logical choice," she argued. "Tandy has already done her worst to me. *You're* the one we've always been worried about."

"I didn't get off all that easy, you know." He stacked her plate on top of his and got up.

She knew he was right. She rose, too. "Let me do that."

"I've got it," he said, and headed to the kitchen.

"Stubborn," she said as he loaded the dirty dishes into her dishwasher. "*Mule* headed."

"Pot calling kettle black," he said as he returned. He wrapped his arms around her shoulders and held her close.

"Well," she said, returning the embrace. "I don't like it, that's all."

"I haven't liked it since I was fourteen years old," he said.

"Neither have I."

"So it's high time we put an end to it. Okay?"

"That's fine," she said. "I'm all for it. But not like this."

"It's the only way there is," he said. "Our only other option is to drive to California and storm the Institute."

She chuckled. "Now there's a mental picture. Two geezers on horseback, with pikes."

"Lances."

She looked up at him, one eyebrow way up. "You use the weapon you want, and I'll use the weapon I want."

He laughed at that, and guided her to the couch. "I have noted your objections," he said as they sat. "*Both* of them. I'll let you know how the meeting went as soon as it's over."

"You had better," she said, and sighed. "I almost wish you hadn't told me. I won't get a wink of sleep tonight."

"Oh?" he said.

His tone of voice caught her off-guard. Slowly, she looked up at him. "I..."

She got no farther. His lips met hers and lingered there, leaving her out of breath. Her hands slipped under his shirt and moved of their own volition, exploring familiar terrain – his back, his torso, the sides of his face.

"I should've shaved," he said, making her giggle.

"It's not so bad," she said. "I should have..."

He put a finger to her lips. "None of that, now."

She kissed his finger. "None of what?"

He held her gaze. "You know."

She did know. That was *her* ability, after all – knowing how the past drove people to do what they did in the present. She knew the years hadn't been kind to either one of them; she was fat and he was balding. But it went beyond mere physical mileage. Thanks to what Tandy did to them as teens, neither of them, as adults, had ever been able to trust. Vulnerability – the kind that allows people to open up to others and form close relationships – hadn't been in either's emotional toolkit. Not for a very long time.

"Don't shut me out," he whispered. "Please. I need you, Janis." He swallowed. "I love you."

That door deep inside her – the one that had swung open briefly a few days before – opened wide, and all the pain and fear and longing she'd been hiding away behind it came rushing out. But nestled between the layers of pain, like a grain of sand in an oyster, was a tiny spark of hope. And it flared when she said, "I never stopped loving you."

Her spark lit his. And while their mutual fire didn't quite consume them, the two of them – geezers though they were – managed to build a respectable bonfire.

California, 1976

Chapter 19

Jan dreaded his training sessions with Tandy these days – and not only because she kept demanding that he do increasingly difficult tricks with his talent that were, frankly, beyond him. He hated to disappoint her – not because he was the sort of guy who groveled, because he never had been, but because when she was disappointed, she sneered and rained insults on him. If she'd insisted that he grovel before her, it would have been easier to take than her constant belittling. He had always known he wasn't perfect. She didn't have to keep reminding him.

Yet as much as she seemed to love to cut him down to size, she still wanted to get into his pants at every opportunity. He couldn't figure it out. If he was as worthless as she said he was, why did she want to have sex with him all the time? It was like the only thing perfect about him was his penis.

He hated Tandy. She humiliated him on a daily basis and she didn't care who saw it. He knew it made the recording techs uncomfortable. Sometimes he could sort of detach from what she was saying to him – kind of float above it, as if the abuse was happening to someone else – and at those times, he would see the tech in the booth shield his eyes and shift in his seat, as if he too wanted to escape.

Why did they stick around? Was it for the money? Or was Tandy screwing them, too, just like she had been screwing Carruthers for years and years?

Carruthers. He was another accomplice. Sometimes he would be in the booth with Tandy when she went into one of her tirades. He would stand as still as stone through it all. Never once did he stand up to her or take Jan's side. Jan hated him, too.

The only person in the whole place who was on his side – the only one he could trust – was Janis. She was *livid* on his behalf. And on the handful of occasions when he couldn't escape Tandy's attentions and his body betrayed him, Janis was always there to talk him in off the ledge.

Figuratively speaking, of course. There were no ledges high enough to allow him to do anything drastic to ease his pain – the Institute building was only a few floors high. The most he could do was break a few bones in the fall.

Not that the thought of suicide occurred to him. Not very often, anyway.

There was one day, though, when he thought he might have someone else in his corner. It was after Tandy had lit into him with a particularly vicious bout of name-calling. He had hung his head and agreed with her assessment, as he always did, because he'd learned that if he argued with her, it only made things worse. At last the hour was over and he was able to leave. But as he dragged himself through the door, he heard the tech on duty – a new guy named Jake, nice looking, with brown hair and a bushy, reddish mustache – say to Tandy, "Why don't you lay off the kid?"

Jan froze. He didn't know whether to run and hide, or rush back into the room and wave madly at the guy to keep his mouth shut. Nothing good could come of this, he knew.

"Who asked for your opinion?" Tandy said hotly.

"Nobody," said Jake. "You sure as hell didn't. But I'm familiar with operators like you, and what you're doing to him is terrible."

How was he hearing this? Had Tandy accidentally left her P.A. mic on, or had Jake turned it on deliberately?

"Oh?" said Tandy, her voice as cold as ice. Jan shuddered. "What do you suggest I do instead?"

"How about encouraging him once in a while? Maybe give him a compliment for trying so hard to please you."

"And what would that accomplish?" she demanded.

"For one thing, maybe he'd stop looking at you like he wants to kill you." That must have left Tandy speechless, because Jake continued,

"You haven't seen it, I know. He's good at doing it behind your back. But you're not doing yourself any favors with the way you're treating him. My grandmother always said you catch more flies with honey than with vinegar."

"Your grandmother is irrelevant," Tandy hissed. "I am not trying to catch flies! I am trying to build an empire, and I need his talent to do it!"

"An empire?" Jake said. "That's a laugh. Dr. Empress Tandy. What do you plan to be empress of?"

"The world," she said evenly. "With these two kids under my control, I'll have everything I need to run things my way – and to ruin anyone who stands in my way. Like you," she sneered. "Get out. And don't come back."

At that, Jake laughed aloud. "You can't fire me. Uncle Ray won't let you."

"Get out!" she screamed.

Jan didn't stay around to hear the rest.

Unfortunately, Jake must not have had the kind of pull with Uncle Ray that he thought he did. Jan never saw him in the booth again, and Janis said he never worked on any of her sessions, either.

Janis would always shake her head when Jan told her the kind of stuff Tandy said to him. She was hard on Janis, too, but it never rose to the level of vitriol that she spewed at Jan. No, Janis's shouting matches with Tandy had a completely different quality.

Jan heard one of them once. He was passing by the training room while the two of them were going at it. Tandy was screaming at Janis, trying to get her to visualize some poor sap's bank balance or something, and Janis just went off on her. "This is not in my skill set, and you know it!" Janis yelled so loudly that Jan could hear her through the closed door. "And anyway, this has got to be illegal!"

"What do you know about what's illegal and what's not?" Tandy yelled back.

"I know plenty!"

Tandy's tone turned suspicious. "How? Who's been feeding you information?"

"Oh, for God's sake," Janis said. About ten seconds later, she yanked the door open. Her eyes flew open when she saw Jan standing in the hallway.

Tandy's voice was much louder, now that the closed door wasn't muffling it. "Get your ass back in there! I'm not through with you!"

"Not a chance. I've had enough of you today," Janis tossed over her shoulder. She looked away from Jan and marched off toward their quarters.

"That's it! I've had it with your attitude! I'm throwing you out!" Tandy screamed.

That got Jan's attention. Tandy had never threatened to kick *him* out of the Institute.

But that wasn't the end of it. Hearing no response from Janis, Tandy fired her final salvo, so loud that it echoed in the corridor. "You little bitch! You'll never have him! He's *mine*!"

Stunned, he followed his friend.

He found Janis slamming things around in the kitchen. "There is *never* anything decent to eat around here," she said, slamming the refrigerator door.

"Has she said that to you before?" he asked.

"What? That she'd kick me out? Sure. About twice a week." She opened random cabinet doors and banged them shut.

"Because she's never said it to me," he said.

Janis froze, then stared at him. "Really? Never?"

"No. Not once."

She turned back to the fridge. "I guess she wants to keep you around for the sex, then." She grabbed an apple from the crisper bin and shut the door. Then she shook it in his face. "This is not chocolate. Do you hear me? Not. Chocolate." She crunched down fiercely on the fruit.

"There's no sex for her to keep me around *for*," he said. "You know that."

"Yeah, I know." She maneuvered past him to get out to the lounge. "The whole thing just pisses me off, that's all." She pulled a cushion off the couch one-handed and sat cross-legged atop it.

He sat on the couch's remaining seat cushion. "And it's getting worse."

"And we both know why," she said. "It's because I'm turning eighteen in a month. And you're right after me." She took another bite of apple. "She's running out of time to weaponize us."

"So," Jan said. "I don't think you heard the last thing she said."

"There was more?"

"Yeah. She said you could never have … someone."

She nodded. "You. She meant you."

"I thought so." He paused. "Have you ever …?"

"What? Like, *challenged* her for you or something?" She rolled her eyes. "Of course not. She made it all up in that diseased brain of hers."

Jan wasn't sure whether that made him feel better or not. "Okay," he said. "I guess we just have to stick it out for one more month."

"Two, at most," she agreed. "And then we can bust out of here, and nobody can stop us."

Chapter 20

Janis yawned and stirred the dregs of her cereal with her spoon. Why Tandy had scheduled her latest doctor appointment so damn early, she had no idea.

Jan came out of his room and blinked when he saw her. "You're up early. And done with breakfast already. What's going on?"

"Another doctor appointment. I can't *wait* 'til I turn eighteen. Then I can make my own appointments at a much more reasonable hour." She yawned again.

"Just three more weeks," he said encouragingly.

"Yeah. Seems like a lifetime." She stood up and headed for the kitchen with her bowl. "Let me know what happens in class."

Jan snorted. "Nothing, probably. This guy never gives us substantive work unless both of us are there. I'll probably be doing independent reading again."

"Have you noticed that our tutors are kind of letting us skate lately?" she said. "Like they know we're almost out of here?"

He nodded. "Yeah. It's like they don't care anymore."

"That makes two of us," she said.

"Three," he said. "Three of us."

She grinned. "See ya at lunch." Then she left their quarters and headed down the hall to Tandy's office.

The doctor's door was open, and a rectangle of light spilled out onto the hallway carpet. Janis stopped, struck by a memory – her own, for once – of an early morning several years before. She had come by to drop off a paper before Tandy arrived for the day, and overheard Tandy and Mr. Carruthers having sex in her office. That was the morning she'd discovered Tandy wanted to use her and Jan as some kind of weapon.

It wasn't until later that Jan had found out Tandy wanted to use their talents to help her with some nefarious scheme to take over the world or something.

Yeah, well, if the not-so-good doctor was going to do it, she was going to have to get a move on. In just a few more weeks, both Jan and Janis would turn eighteen. Then they would be adults, and Tandy would have to let them go.

The thought lightened her steps. She was practically skipping when she rounded the corner into Tandy's office. But then she stopped cold.

Usually, when Janis was to see the doctor, Tandy escorted her to the medical lab, which was in a different wing of the Institute. The lab wasn't always staffed, but it had examination rooms stocked with medical supplies – tongue depressors, rolls of gauze, and so on. There, they would meet the M.D. who was to do the exam. Tandy would hand her off to him – it was usually a male doctor – and disappear.

Today, however, several people in white lab coats were with Tandy in her office. Janis decided the one with the drastic comb-over and the officious air must be the doctor. She had never seen him before.

"This is the patient?" Must-Be-Doctor said to Tandy.

"Yes, this is Janis," Tandy said. "Janis, you are to go with these people this morning."

"Okay," she said slowly. "What's this all about? Why are there so many of you?"

One of the other medical people stepped forward with a blood pressure cuff. He affixed it to her arm and began pumping the little black ball, using a stethoscope to listen to something in the crook of her arm. "One ten over seventy," he told the third person, who nodded and made a note on a clipboard. Stethoscope Guy turned back to her. "Did you eat breakfast this morning?"

Janis frowned. "Of course. I always eat breakfast. Why?"

Stethoscope Guy turned to Must-Be-Doctor, who glared at Tandy. Tandy glared in turn at Janis. "I told you, nothing by mouth after midnight."

Janis shook her head. "No, you didn't. You never said anything like that. All you said was to meet you here at six a.m."

Tandy fluttered a hand. "Well, it doesn't really matter, does it?"

Stethoscope Guy said, "We'll hope not. But if she vomits while under anesthesia, she could choke."

"Anesthesia!" Janis said. "What's happening? What are you planning to do to me?"

Clipboard Woman walked up to her and stroked her shoulder. "There, there," she crooned. "It's all right. When you wake up, everything will be fine."

"But ..." She gasped. While the woman was distracting her, Stethoscope Guy stuck a needle in her arm. Janis yelled and thrashed, but the woman held her in a tight hug while the man hooked up the needle to a bag of fluid on a pole.

Suddenly she felt dizzy. The woman guided her to a chair and helped her sit.

The last thing Janis remembered as she slipped under was Must-Be-Doctor saying, "I don't like this, Denise. Not one bit."

Janis was woozy when she awoke. The room she was in was completely unfamiliar to her – it looked kind of like one of the exam rooms in the medical wing, but it was laid out differently. There was a closet door in one corner – that was not a feature of any of the exam rooms she'd ever been in – and she was in a regular bed instead of on an exam bench.

Well, maybe it wasn't a *regular* bed. There was a box with buttons on it – Up, Down, and Call.

And it seemed awfully noisy out in the hallway. People kept passing by and an intercom kept repeating doctors' names with the word, "STAT!"

She tried to sit up, but it felt like her midsection was on fire. Gingerly she pulled back the bedclothes and pulled up the ugly nightgown someone had dressed her in. A bandage stretched across the width of her lower abdomen.

Scared, she cried out, but it didn't seem to make a dent in the din from the hallway. The only thing within reach was the button box. She hit Call, then let her hand drop to the mattress.

She must have slept, because the next thing she remembered was a woman in a nurse's uniform coming into the room. She knew this wasn't the woman with the clipboard from Tandy's office. And once she remembered that, she remembered the rest of the happenings on that strange morning.

"Ah, we're awake," the nurse said with a smile.

"Where am I?" Janis said. She tried again to sit up and winced.

"At County Hospital. Don't try to sit up – let the bed do the work. Here." The nurse pressed the Up button, a motor whirred to life, and the head of the bed raised slowly. In a few moments, the nurse decided the incline was sufficient and released the button. Then she plumped up a pillow and slid it expertly behind Janis's head. "Now if you decide you'd rather lie down again, push the other button. And if you need me, hit Call, just like you did before. Do you want something for the pain?"

Janis grimaced. "I guess. Yeah, that would be good. Do you have any Tylenol?"

The nurse laughed. "We have something better than Tylenol. I'll be right back." She turned to go.

"Wait," Janis called, and the nurse turned back. "What happened to me? Why am I here?"

The nurse frowned. "You had your tubes tied, honey."

"*What?*"

131

The nurse backed toward the door. "I'd better let your mother know you're awake. And I'll be back with your medication in a minute."

"My *mother?*" she cried out. But the nurse was gone, and anyway it hurt too much to yell. Her thoughts whirling, she sank back on the pillow and waited for the nurse to return.

You had your tubes tied. Janis knew what it meant in general terms – she wouldn't be able to have a baby – but that didn't mean it made sense. Her periods were normal. None of the doctors she had seen had ever told her that pregnancy would hurt her. She didn't need *any* kind of surgery that she knew of. What was going on? And why on earth was her *mother* here? She hadn't seen her since the day she said goodbye to her and Gigi in the Institute's lobby.

The woman who walked through the door wasn't her mother, though – it was Tandy. "Hello, Janis," she said with her mechanical smile. "How are you feeling?"

She ignored the question. She was sure Tandy didn't care about the answer, anyway. "Where's my mother?" she said instead. "The nurse said my mother was here."

"Your mother?" Tandy laughed. "What would *she* be doing here? The nurse must have thought *I* was your mother."

"Because you were waiting for me to wake up."

"Precisely." Another fake smile.

Janis's belly was beginning to throb. "The nurse also said I'd had my tubes tied."

Tandy stopped smiling. "I will have a word with your doctor. The staff shouldn't be allowed to be so free with such information."

"Why not? It's my body. Shouldn't I be told what's happening to me?"

"No," Tandy said firmly. "You're still a child. You wouldn't understand."

Janis would have laughed if her belly had hurt any less. "I'll be eighteen in three weeks."

132

"Yes, I know. Which is why this had to be done now."

This conversation was getting more and more bizarre. Janis opened her mouth to ask another question, but the nurse interrupted them. She bustled in with a glass of water and a tiny paper cup. "Having a nice visit, are we?" she asked brightly. "Here, honey, take this and drink every bit of water in this glass." The nurse stood by while Janis obeyed. "There you go. I'll be by with your lunch in a little while – only broth and Jell-O for now, I'm afraid. You can have a regular dinner at home tonight." The nurse looked at Tandy. "She's very lucky. The surgeon was able to do the procedure laparoscopically." She turned back to Janis. "In the old days, you'd have had a big old scar right down the middle of your belly" – she drew a vertical line on her own abdomen – "and you would have been our guest for a *week*." She smiled at them both. "Well, I'll get out of your way. Call me if you need me," she said to Janis, and made her way out.

"Close the door," Janis said.

"Actually," said Tandy, "I need to be going, too."

"We're not done with this conversation," Janis said.

"Oh, I think we are." There was that ghastly smile again. "You do want me to take you home this afternoon, don't you?"

It was hard, but Janis kept her lips firmly zipped. She did need to go back to the Institute, if only for Jan's sake. And she had no doubt Tandy would abandon her upon the slightest provocation.

"I thought you'd see reason," Tandy said, and walked out.

Tears of frustration leaked from the corners of her eyes. There was nothing else she could do. She pushed the Down button on the bed and waited for the pain medication to take her away.

Chapter 21

It was nearly dinnertime and Jan was uneasy. He hadn't seen Janis since breakfast – she hadn't showed up at lunch or for their afternoon class – and now she was about to miss dinner, too. He sat in the lounge, waiting for her, but trying not to be obvious about it. Although anyone watching him on the security camera would have known he was distracted – he spent more time looking at the door to their quarters, willing it to open, than he did reading his book.

At last, the door did open, and Janis walked through it.

"There you are!" he called out in a teasing voice. "Where have you been all day?"

She didn't reply – just continued walking slowly toward the couch. He noticed then that she was holding her belly in an awkward way.

"Hey," he said. "What's wrong? What happened?"

She sagged onto the edge of the couch and dropped a plastic bag on the floor beside her. Her reply was so soft that he almost couldn't hear it. "They tied my tubes."

His eyes flew open. "What?"

She wrapped both arms around her belly and began to cry.

Instantly, he was next to her, holding her, letting her tears soak his shirt. "Why, though? Did anybody tell you?"

"No," she said. "Tandy won't tell me." And in short bursts of words punctuated by sobs, she told him everything that had happened.

The more she talked, the angrier Jan became. "If she won't tell *you,* you can be damn sure she'll tell *me,*" he vowed fiercely.

"No, Jan, don't," she said, clutching at his collar. "Just let it go."

"How *can* I?" he said.

"Just let it go," she repeated. "The surgeon told me just before *she* picked me up that it's not the kind that can be reversed. There's nothing either of us can do about it."

"Except wait 'til we can legally walk out of here."

She nodded. "She said … she said that's why this had to be done now."

"Oh, God." He held her tightly. "It was her last chance to hurt you."

She looked up at him again. "That's the other reason you can't confront her."

"What do you mean?"

"If she'd go this far to hurt *me*, what would she do to *you*?" She let go of her stomach long enough to grab his arm and hold on. "I can't let that happen. I need for you to be safe." Her head sank down onto his shoulder again. "One of us needs to be safe. And it's too late for me."

A service worker came in with containers of food, placed them in the kitchen, and walked out. After the woman left, Jan said, "Dinner's here. Are you hungry? Can you eat something?"

"I think I'm supposed to," she said. "They gave me pain pills. And a sheet of instructions." She reached for the plastic bag on the floor and winced.

Jan retrieved the bag for her. She pulled out a set of stapled pages titled *Post-Surgical Instructions for Tubal Ligation* and handed it to him. Then she fished around for the plastic medicine vial.

"Are you supposed to take them with food?" he asked.

"It doesn't say." She handed the vial to him, too.

He studied the label. Percocet was the name of the drug. "You should probably try to eat something anyway. Did you get lunch?"

She made a face. "Gross beef broth that I didn't finish. And green Jell-O and apple juice."

"Sounds yummy," he said, which got a weak laugh out of her.

"Come on." He helped her get seated at the table, although she probably could have managed it herself, and then fetched both their dinners from the kitchen.

She gave him a grateful smile as he set her plate down. "You're so good to me."

His heart swelled. He stroked her long, blond hair, then took his own seat.

She managed a few bites, but he could tell her heart wasn't in it. "I think I'm going to turn in," she said. "Oh, I'm supposed to tell you: Tandy canceled our classes for the rest of the week. The doctor told her I shouldn't go, and I said it was hardly fair to make you take notes for both of us for a whole week."

"Thank you," he said.

"Well, it *wouldn't* be fair."

"I would have done it, though," he said. "But I'd rather stay here and take care of you."

The smile she gave him was worth whatever she was about to put him through.

But she turned out to be an undemanding invalid. She spent most of the day after her surgery sleeping, but after that, she generally sat up in the lounge with him. They talked for hours, about everything and nothing. Jan looked back on that week later as a blessing, in a way, even though what had prompted it was so horrible.

Best of all, Tandy canceled training sessions for both of them for the week, too. Neither one of them had to see her at all, which made it a *very* good week.

Janis's mood went up and down. She was sore for the first few days after the operation, but that gradually went away. She found she was able to stop taking the pills before the week was up – but she kept them just in case. Just in case of what, she didn't feel the need to specify to herself. But she felt better knowing they were there, in the drawer of her nightstand.

To be honest, she spent so much time out in the lounge because when she was alone in her room, her thoughts crowded too close around her: everything from why Tandy had ordered the surgery to what she would do once she left the Institute. Her "graduation" was only a few short weeks away, but she had no idea what would happen then. She had nowhere to go and no one to contact. She supposed she could eventually find the overpass she and her mother used to sleep under and ask around, but she thought contacting Gigi would be safer. The problem was she didn't know Gigi's address or phone number. And she didn't want to count on Tandy just handing it over to her. Hell, Tandy might insist that she leave all her things behind, including the clothes on her back.

And too, she resented Tandy's presumption in setting up the surgery. Janis had never thought about whether she wanted to have children, but now that it was certain she couldn't, it was on her mind all the time. It was like having a door slammed in your face before you even realized it was open. Sometimes, lying in bed, she would cry over the children she would never have a chance to bear and raise. She knew for sure she would have been a better mother than her own mother had been; for starters, she would never hand her kids over to some monster to raise. If she could have kids. Which she couldn't.

The pain pills gave her odd dreams. She dreamed that her mother actually *had* come to the hospital to see her, but her hospital room looked completely different than it had in real life, and anyway it turned out it was Gigi who showed up for her, not Mama. Mama was too sick to come, Gigi said, and Janis replied that Mama was always and forever too sick to take care of her.

The least pleasant dreams were the ones Tandy showed up in. Usually she was a shadowy, menacing presence; the only reason Janis knew it was her was because she recognized her voice. She would always whisper terrible things to her: she was a lousy student and a rotten girl in general; she had no talent to speak of and the little she had was useless;

she should have been thrown out into the cold years ago. Janis would wake up from these dreams in a sweat. She always had a hard time falling back to sleep afterward. In fact, it was usually after one of these dreams that she would go out to the lounge to find Jan.

Only once did she dream of Jan, and it was so realistic – and so erotic – that she was sure he had come into her room and made love to her while she slept. She could feel his warm breath on her cheek and the texture of his skin under her fingers. But no, he'd been in his room the whole time, or so he claimed.

Did it matter to *him* that she could no longer bear children? She didn't know. That was one thing they never talked about.

The more resigned Janis became to what had happened to her, the angrier it made Jan. He wasn't mad at her, of course. None of it was her fault. But he was mad as hell at Tandy, and that anger was destined to find an outlet somehow.

Janis had gotten into the habit of taking a nap after lunch. She'd find herself yawning, then proclaim herself a big baby for being so tired. Then Jan would reassure her that she had been through a lot and if she needed more sleep to recover, she should take advantage of the opportunity – there would be no time for napping once classes resumed. She would then agree and head off to her room for an hour or so.

And then he'd sit and stew, debating whether to confront Tandy or abide by Janis's wishes and keep his nose out of it.

Except his nose was already in it. Or it might be. Tandy could have attacked Janis as a backhanded way to get to him. Sure, Tandy and Janis were always arguing, but it seemed like he was generally what they argued about.

There was no way to know for sure until she explained herself. And while she had expressly told Janis the discussion was closed, she hadn't told *him*.

Round and round his thoughts went, getting him more and more worked up.

Finally, on day five of their week off from everything, Jan had had enough. He played his part in Janis's little afternoon ritual, gave her a few minutes to settle into bed, and then let himself out of their quarters.

Just outside Tandy's doorway, he stopped and listened. The door was open and her lights were on – he could tell by the bright spot on the hallway carpet. If she was in there, she was being awfully quiet – but it also meant no one else was in there with her.

Her phone rang and someone picked it up. It was Tandy, obviously, because she had a brief conversation with whoever was on the other end of the line and then hung up.

He figured that was his cue. He strode to the doorway, crossed his arms, leaned on the jamb, and glowered at her.

It took a few moments for her to look up. "Yes?" she said, poker-faced.

He was silent.

She turned back to the file on her desk. "As you can see, I'm busy. If you have something to say, say it."

"All right, I will. Why?"

She looked up again. "Why what?"

"Don't play games with me, Tandy," he said, deliberately dropping the honorific for the first time in all his dealings with her. "You know what this is about."

"I might or might not. Why don't you refresh my memory?"

He knew this wouldn't be easy, but he hadn't expected it to be this hard. "Okay, fine," he said. He took two steps into her office and stood just behind her guest chair. "On Monday, Janis left very early for a doctor appointment. Except it wasn't just a run-of-the-mill appointment. You abducted her and took her to have her tubes tied."

Tandy laughed. "Abducted? Really, Jan, I expect this level of drama from her, not from you."

"What would _you_ call it?"

"She's my _ward_," Tandy said evenly. "As are you. Your parents all signed over their legal rights to raise you when they left you in my care."

Jan was too shocked to speak. _Wards? We're_ wards _of hers?_

"I cannot, by definition, abduct you. I have the legal right to make all decisions that I believe are in your best interests – including medical decisions. And I believed it was in Janis's best interests to have a tubal ligation."

"Why?" he demanded.

"Because she's not competent to raise a child," Tandy said. "She is mentally unstable. If she were allowed to become pregnant, her mental condition would be detrimental to the child's welfare."

"You're joking," he said. "You _have_ to be joking. You did this to her because she talks back to you?"

Tandy leveled a look at him. "I made the determination based on her so-called talent."

"That doesn't make any sense," he said. "Then I should be incompetent to raise a child, too. Why haven't you had _me_ sterilized?"

She got up from her desk and closed the door. Then she stood nose-to-nose with him and said, through gritted teeth, "Because I want to have sex with you, and you keep running away from me." She grabbed his arms. "Do you think I don't know what the two of you are planning? You're just dying to get away from here. Don't deny it! I've heard you – 'I can't _wait_ 'til we're eighteen!' Because then you can leave and I can't do anything about it!" She shook him. "You're plotting to deprive me of my army!"

"Your army?" was all Jan could manage.

"For years now, I've been waiting for the two of you to have children. To make _more_ of you. I've dreamed of having a whole tribe of talented children – all under my complete control. With that kind of foreknowledge of every possible situation, I could be rich! I could rule the world!" She shook him again. "But the two of you wouldn't cooperate! And now it's too late!"

"You're insane," he said.

"Don't you see?" she went on. "I had to do it. I couldn't let the two of you go out into the world to make your *own* army. Those children are mine by right!" She reached for his belt buckle. "And I am going to have them, one way or another!"

"What are you doing? Hey! Hey!" he yelled. "Help!"

"There's no one close enough to hear you scream," she said, and pushed him onto the loveseat.

He told himself later that it was his fault. He was stronger than her. He could have fought her off. He *should* have fought her off.

He was a man, for goodness' sake. Men don't get raped. They can't!

But he had.

And he couldn't bring himself to tell his only friend what had happened. He couldn't burden her with his anguish. She was already in so much pain.

New Mexico

Chapter 22

As was his habit, Jan waited until the last minute to show up for the Project Terraform team meeting. Usually that meant he could stand in the back of the room, stay quiet and unnoticed, and be the first one to slip out when it was over.

But this particular meeting was in a conference room with a big table, and Bennie had made sure the staff knew exactly how many chairs he needed so that everyone would have a seat. As the presenter, Bennie sat next to the videoconference screen with his laptop, the camera trained on him. Everybody else had wisely sat out of range of the camera. The only seat left at the table was right next to Bennie.

Jan was about to pretend he didn't see the open chair, but Bennie waved to him and pointed at it. Sighing, Jan made a mental note to get here really early next time, so he could at least grab the seat closest to the door.

If there was a next time. If what he was planning to do didn't backfire in his face.

A number of his colleagues nodded at him as he made his way down the long, long table. "Good to see you, Jan," said one.

"Welcome to the madness," said another, to general chuckles.

"Yeah, thanks," Jan said with a smile that was just this side of sarcastic. "Looking forward to it." That got a bigger laugh.

"Welcome," Bennie said as he sat down. "Guys, this is Jan Marek. I guess most of you know him – he's been here a long time." Nods all around.

Bennie turned to him. "Did you read the binder I gave you?"

"I did," Jan said.

"The whole thing?"

"Of course."

"Okay, good. Throw it out. Everything has changed."

That got a general round of laughter. Bennie looked around the table. "I'm not joking. Everybody, throw it out. This new client is pushing reset on the whole program. I got word over the weekend. We are to begin work on designing a relay for special type of communications. Something that no one has ever succeeded at creating before." He grinned. "Revolutionary. We will be the first to do it, ever. And I know we are the best team in the world to get it done, and done right." He looked at Jan. "That's why I'm so pleased to have you on board. This is right up your alley."

Jan smiled and nodded, but he had no idea what the guy meant by that. He thought he had been careful *not* to specialize.

A hand went up. "Bennie, are we not able to salvage *any* of the work my team has done over the past nine months?"

"Ah, Jake. Yes, of course. Your part of the project will survive. We will need the hardware you guys have been building, with some modifications to the specs."

Jake began typing on his laptop. "Okay, good. When will we get the new specs?"

"First thing tomorrow. The client is sending them by courier from California."

Jake looked up. "They couldn't email them?"

Bennie shook his head. "Not secure enough."

Jake blew a raspberry. "So these people are into cloak-and-dagger stuff. Great." He shook his head and went back to typing.

"Yes, Rajesh?" Bennie said, indicating a man at the end of the table.

"My team planned to leave for the launch site later this afternoon. Should we cancel our trip?"

Bennie thought for a moment. "Go," he said. "We will still be sending material to Mars. It will be good to have our own assessment of the facilities and how much room NASA can spare us in the cargo hold."

Rajesh exchanged nods with several people at the end of the table. "Okay, thanks," he said to Bennie.

"Jan," Bennie said. "You will be the liaison between the client and our team. You will be responsible for making sure that what they ask for is what we deliver."

"Okay, sure," Jan said, but his stomach dropped to his feet. He had wanted to be involved in this project in order to gather information on the Institute – or rather, on FAE. He never thought he would have to communicate directly with this Jenkins fellow, other than in that parallel universe or whatever it was.

"Good," Bennie said, and fiddled with his computer. "I'm forwarding you the email I got over the weekend."

Jan pulled it up on his phone. The top email in the chain was from Jenkins, and Bennie had covered all of the contents in his opening comments. "This is it?" he asked in disbelief. "This is everything we know?"

"Yep," Bennie said, pulling up a different app. The video screen, previously dark, now sprang to life, and the kid – Antoine Jenkins – appeared on one side of it. Bennie and Jan appeared on the other side.

"Mr. Jenkins, welcome," Bennie said. "Can you hear me?"

"I can," Jenkins replied. "Can you hear me?"

"Yes, we can," Bennie crowed. "We are off to a good start!"

"Ain't technology grand?" Jake muttered.

Jan would have grinned, but he was too busy examining what was behind Jenkins. If he wasn't mistaken, the kid was using Jan's old room at the Institute for an office. He recognized some of the dents and scrapes in the built-in bookshelves as his own work.

"Mr. Jenkins, I am Bennie Deng. We spoke on the phone late last week."

"Right, yeah. I remember you. Did you get my email?"

"I did, and I have taken the liberty of passing it along to my colleague, Jan Marek. He is now the communications liaison for the team."

Jan nodded stiffly. "Mr. Jenkins."

Jenkins looked him over and frowned. "Look, Mr. Deng, I don't know about this. We need to keep a lock on information on this project. It's very sensitive stuff."

"I understand," Bennie said. "Not to worry. Mr. Marek is very trustworthy."

Jenkins looked him over again. "You're new, aren't you?"

Jan allowed the kid to see him bristle slightly. "I've been with Jemez Aerospace for thirty years," he said, deliberately shortening his resume.

"That's not what I ... Look, Bennie. Can I call you Bennie?" Jenkins said.

"I would prefer to keep our relationship formal," said Bennie.

Jan carefully schooled his features. This was not the way Jemez Aerospace had ever done business. Everyone was always on a first-name basis, employees and clients alike. What was going on here?

The kid rolled his eyes, but barely. "Fine. Mr. Deng. I was told by your supervisor that I would be dealing strictly with you."

"And you have – until now. Now you deal with Mr. Marek." Bennie gave him a self-deprecating smile. "Mr. Jenkins, my English is not so good. Much about this project has change now. I find hard to understand. It will be more easy for you to talk to Mr. Marek from now on."

Ah, so, Jan thought, adopting a little pidgin English in his own head. *You don't trust him.*

Jenkins looked none too pleased. "I will have to clear this with my boss," he said. "And I will be following up with your Mr. Abioye, if that's all right with you."

"Sure, sure," Bennie said, nodding and smiling. "I send you Mr. Marek's contact info now. And we wait for your new specs."

Jenkins nodded. He was about to say something else, but Bennie closed the line too fast.

As soon as the big screen went dark, Jake asked what everyone wanted to know. "Are we in a Charlie Chan movie now? What's with the accent, Bennie?"

"The client is changing the rules in the middle of the game," said Bennie. "So I threw a curve ball of my own."

As Bennie spoke, Jan scrolled through the email chain with Jenkins' new rules at the top. Most of the exchanges had occurred over the last couple of days of the previous week. He could see where Bennie had tried to nail the kid down to specifics – manpower, due dates for deliverables, and so on – and Jenkins had continually sidestepped his questions. And then, over the weekend, Jenkins announced that FAE was changing its plans and he wanted Bennie to buy into the change.

"This whole thing smells bad," Jan said, looking up at Bennie.

"I thought so, too."

"You think we should cancel the contract?"

Bennie smiled. "Not yet. I'm not ready to do that yet, and Dan isn't, either."

Someone across the table – Jan thought his name was Clinton – asked, "What if FAE pulls out? Will we still have the contract with NASA?"

"Good question," Jan said. Projects for NASA were the company's bread and butter.

"I believe so," said Bennie. "Dan is reviewing our contract with them on Terraform to make sure." He dropped his voice. "He isn't happy, either. It was his idea to give Jan the title of liaison." He grinned at Jan. "He said you have a good track record with difficult clients. No." He held up a hand. "What he said was you're amazing with them."

"I'll have to thank him for that personal reference," Jan muttered.

"Jan's the Fixer, y'all," Clinton said, to general laughter.

149

"So we shouldn't throw out our briefing books, after all?" Rajesh said with a grin.

"Good point. Keep them for now," Bennie said. "And Rajesh, go ahead with your site visit. Everybody else, hit pause for a day, until we get a look at those new specs."

"The fun never stops," Jake muttered. He closed his laptop and joined the queue at the door.

Jan got up to follow them, but Bennie put a hand on his arm. "Do you have a minute? Dan asked me to stop by after this meeting and brief him. I think he would like to see you, too."

"Sure," Jan said.

The first thing he said to Dan was, "Thanks for the new title. Clinton's calling me the Fixer now."

Dan laughed uproariously at that. "That's good! It suits you." As Jan and Bennie sat, he went on, "I trust the change in leadership went over well?"

Jan looked between the two of them. "Leadership? I thought I was just liaising."

"Of course," Bennie said. "Client management, that's all." To Dan, he said, "Mr. Jenkins didn't appear to be happy with the change."

"Not even a little bit," Jan agreed. "What's his beef, anyway?"

"Your age, I'd guess," Dan said. "I don't know how to break this to you, Jan, but you're old."

"I'm aware of that," said Jan. "Every morning when I try to get out of bed."

The three men laughed. "And Jenkins is a kid, right?"

"That's how I've always thought of him," Jan said.

Dan looked at him quizzically.

"Since we first saw him in the staff meeting the other day," Jan hastened to add. "He seems very young to be a global vice president. Don't you guys think so?"

"Definitely," said Bennie.

"He does weave an amazing tale of bullshit, though," Dan said. "I mean, FAE's proposal seemed plausible when he first approached us. You thought so, too – didn't you, Bennie?"

"Sure," Bennie confirmed. "You and I talked about it. It seemed legit."

"But now with this paranormal stuff…" Dan shook his head. "That's why I was so happy when you volunteered for the project, Jan. These guys might be leading us down the garden path. We need another, clearer head in charge."

Jan nodded thoughtfully. *Leading them down the garden path* sounded like the kid's M.O., all right.

"I know we sort of sprang the task on you," Bennie said. "We're grateful you've been so willing to play along."

"Speaking of playing along." Jan started to snicker. "You should have seen this guy in the meeting," he told Dan, hooking a thumb at Bennie. "He started doing this pidgin English thing. 'Much about this project is change now.'" He delivered the line in Bennie's fake accent.

Dan's mouth dropped open. "You didn't."

"He did!"

Bennie shrugged. "It seemed expedient."

Dan shook his head and laughed. "Okay, you guys. If you're done showing me your comedy routine, I have work to do. Keep me posted on the new specs."

"We'll send you a copy as soon as they arrive," Bennie assured him.

Chapter 23

Janis was on tenterhooks all morning, wondering how Jan's showdown with Antoine Jenkins had gone. She was pretty sure it hadn't gone badly – she hadn't experienced the open-door sensation she had the last time the two of them had gone head-to-head – but "pretty sure" didn't cover all the possible outcomes.

The longer she waited for him to call, the more nervous she got. To distract herself, she went purposefully to one of the computer terminals in the library and looked up the definition for tenterhooks. Her singleness of purpose baffled a class of sophomores whose English teacher was explaining the library's resources to them, and how they might be used in their upcoming research paper. They were further amused when Mrs. Fowler, the rotund librarian, sat back in her chair and exclaimed, "Of course!"

"'Of course' what, Mrs. Fowler?" asked Tomasina, the desk assistant that hour.

"Tenterhooks," she informed the girl, "were used in olden times to help woolen cloth keep its shape. The hooks were fastened to a big frame called a tenter, and the edges of the cloth were attached to these tenterhooks so the cloth wouldn't shrink as it dried."

"Okay," the girl said slowly. "And that's relevant how?"

"Because I was just thinking about how I – that is, about how a person is said to be on tenterhooks when they're anxious." She regarded Tomasina's tolerant smile. "The phrase just occurred to me, that's all."

She shook her head slightly. "If you say so," she said, and went back to removing the old periodicals from their plastic jackets and putting in the new ones.

"I'm not nervous about anything, if that's what you're wondering," Janis went on, in perhaps too loud a voice. Now several of the sophomores in the back of the tour group were paying more attention to her than to their teacher.

"Bah," she said, and got up out of her chair. She was about to head back to her office – it was nearly lunchtime – when the one of the double doors opened and a smiling Jan walked in.

"Fancy meeting you here," he said when he reached her.

"Why didn't you call?" she demanded in return. "I've been so …" She cast a glance at Tomasina, who was studiously ignoring her, and glared at the sophomores until they stopped staring at Jan and turned their attention back to their teacher. "Come on," she hissed, grabbing Jan's arm and practically towing him to her office.

She shut the door behind them both, then crossed her arms and waited.

"I'm sorry," he said, eyes downcast. "I didn't mean to worry you. I'm just not used to reporting to anybody." He looked up at her through his eyelashes.

She half-smiled and relented. "Oh, it's all right. I'm sorry I got upset with you. I was just …"

"Worried," he supplied. "You were worried last night when I told you what I was planning to do. I should have remembered."

"Oh, stop. I've already forgiven you." She swept a pile of books off her guest chair so he could sit down. "Tea?"

"No, thanks."

"Well, *I* need some." She retrieved a gallon jug of water from under her desk, poured a mugful, and placed her contraband immersion water heater in the mug. Then she turned her chair to face him. Her hands were folded – one elbow on the desk and the other on the arm of her chair – and her feet were crossed at the ankles.

He had a sudden memory of a much younger Janis, sitting cross-legged on a couch cushion and wearing that same expectant look. "I love you," he blurted.

Her expression softened. "I love you, too. Now tell me about the meeting."

"FAE is trying to pull a fast one on us," he said.

"Oh? How so?"

He told her about how vague Antoine Jenkins had been to Bennie, and about the sudden pivot over the weekend to something completely different. "And we still don't know what that is," he said. "Jenkins is sending the new specs by courier overnight. He says they're too sensitive to be put in an email."

Janis unplugged the heater, removed it from her cup, and placed it on a saucer to cool. "I've been hearing good things about email encryption," she said, dunking a tea bag in her hot water.

"And we have an app that will do that," Jan said. "But apparently it's not good enough for this kid."

"Huh," she said. "You sure you don't want any tea?"

"Nah. I came to take you to lunch, to be honest."

She perked up. "Oh. That would be nice."

"Can you get away?"

"For how long?"

He raised his hands, palms up, and spread them wide. "As long as you want. I'm sprung from work for the afternoon. With the FAE project on hold 'til we get the new specs, I have nothing to do. Dan said it was okay if I worked a half-day today."

A slow smile spread across her face. "I can't remember the last time I played hooky." She sipped her tea. "And oddly enough, I have nothing on my calendar this afternoon, either."

"It's kismet," he said.

"Except now I have this tea to finish." She looked askance at the contents of her mug. "And it's my favorite."

Jan sat back and crossed his long legs, one ankle atop the opposite knee. "Take your time. We've got all day."

Their lunch conversation circled back at last to the meeting that morning. "I guess you didn't get anywhere with Jenkins," Janis said.

"There wasn't time. The portion of the meeting he attended was pretty short. He was definitely knocked off his stride when Bennie told him he had to start dealing with me."

"I still don't understand why."

"Why Bennie said that, or why it bothered him?"

Janis leaned forward. "Do you think maybe he knows who you are?"

"I keep telling you no," said Jan. "He doesn't. No, the operative theory is that the kid doesn't want to deal with an old fart like me. It puts him at a disadvantage."

"You're an authority figure," she said, nodding.

"Essentially. I thought about it on the drive over here. If he's been under Tandy's thumb for any length of time, you and I both know he's going to want total control of the situation – because he doesn't have that kind of control with her. *She* controls *him*."

"Right."

"So the last thing he wants is someone else ordering him around. Even if it's only in his head."

"I don't think that's it," she said, frowning. "I … hmm."

"What is it?"

"I had a sense of him." She shook her head. "It's gone now."

Jan sat up straighter and took her hand. "You mean here? Now?"

"Oh!" She waved the hand he wasn't clutching. "No, silly. His *past*. I had a brief glimpse of his *past*." She smiled at him. "I'm not in any danger right now."

He sighed and relaxed his grip. "You had me worried there for a second."

"Now you know how my morning went. Paybacks are hell." She grinned evilly.

"Touché," he said with a rueful smile. "Did you get anything useful?"

155

"Maybe," she said. "It seemed to be about the first time he met Tandy." She closed her eyes and concentrated, then shook her head. "There's not much there. But it seems like he was older when he met her than you were."

"How much older? Teenager older? Young adult older?"

She shook her head again. "I only got a glimpse."

"Old enough to sleep with?"

She burst out laughing. "Jan! She's eighty years old if she's a day! It's not like she could get a baby out of him." She saw him wince. "I'm sorry. That was in poor taste."

He shrugged. "It's not a big deal. It all happened a lifetime ago."

"But the scars don't go away," she said. "Have you ever talked to anyone about it?"

"Other than you?" he said. "No. Of course not."

She sighed. "I'd tell you what a bad idea that is, but then I'd have to confess that I've never talked to a therapist about my trauma, either."

He squeezed her hand. "We're quite a pair, aren't we?"

"We are indeed." They shared a quiet moment. Then she said, "I'm still not clear on one thing. When Bennie told Antoine he'd have to communicate with you in the future, what did he say?"

"He said he'd take it up with Dan," said Jan.

"I'm hearing an *and* in the tone of your voice," she said.

"He also needs to clear it with Tandy."

Janis's heart seemed to stop. "Oh, Jan. Please tell me Antoine doesn't know your name."

"Of course he does. Bennie gave it to him."

Janis sat back in shock. "How can you be so matter-of-fact about this? You know what it means!"

It was clearly just now dawning on Jan what it meant. "Oh. Oh, shit."

"'Oh, shit' is right," she said. "As soon as Antoine gives her your name, she's going to be able to find us."

His mouth set in a line. "We'll just have to be ready for her, that's all." He had never let go of her hand. Now he sat forward and put his other hand on top of their joined ones. "We're not kids anymore, Janis. We're talented; she's not. The only power she has over us is the power we grant her."

She nodded. Then with a sigh, she said, "It was so nice, not being worried for a minute."

Silicon Valley

Chapter 24

"Shit," Antoine muttered.

"Something wrong, boss?" Simone called from her desk in the lobby.

"Yeah. Maybe. I'm not sure." He walked out to her desk. His office was beginning to feel a little claustrophobic, and he couldn't tell whether it was because of Bennie Deng's demeanor or the way the new guy – the old guy – anyway, the *other* guy seemed to look right through him.

She turned her chair toward him. "Sounds like the meeting didn't go the way you planned."

"Not exactly, no." He took a moment to appreciate her look today. The golden extensions were gone, and in their place she had a braided updo going on. The hairstyle seemed to lengthen her neck and give her a regal air. *Queen*, he thought abruptly. *Or goddess.* He shook his head. He didn't need the distraction right now.

"What happened?"

He ran his fingers through his spiky dreads as he paced in front of her desk. "I think maybe Deng is on to us. He's handed me off to another guy in the company. Used bad English as an excuse."

She stared at him, bristling. "Yours?"

"No, no – *his*." Antoine laughed and shook his head. "Guy's got a thick Chinese accent, although it seems to come and go whenever it suits him."

"So this new guy," she prompted.

He shook his head again. "I don't know about him, Mony. He's an old white guy. Way older than anybody else I've dealt with there. And he gives me the creeps. He spent the whole meeting not looking at me."

"Like you weren't there? Or like you weren't important?"

He shrugged. "Neither one. I don't know. It was just weird, that's all." He turned and paced back. "And I'm annoyed, to be honest. I spent all that time working my magic on Abioye, and he handed me off to Deng. Then I worked on Deng, and now he's handed me off to this new guy. The more people's heads I have to play with, the harder the illusion gets to maintain."

He blew out a breath and stopped in front of her desk. "Anyway, I still have to fly out there tomorrow and hand off the new plans to them, and I'm sure Abioye and Deng will make themselves scarce. I'll have to deal with the creepy old guy, one way or another."

"Sounds like you're not looking forward to it," she said.

"Not even a little bit." He tilted his head. A crazy idea was forming in his mind. "Hey, do you have anything pressing going on tomorrow?"

"No, not at all. I was going to work on the filing, but I can put that off again. Why?"

"I'd like for you to come with me," he said.

Her eyes sparkled. "Are you thinking of providing them a little more misdirection?"

"Yeah, kind of," he said with a smile. "Plus it would be good to get out of here for a day, don't you think?" He glanced around the spacious office. "Does it ever feel like the walls are closing in on you in here?"

"No," she replied. "But I'm not under the same kind of pressure you are."

He didn't really hear her. He was thinking of the escape he was plotting. "Yeah. Yeah, I think that's the ticket. A quick flight, maybe a late lunch at a Mexican place in Albuquerque, and then we can drive up to Los Alamos." He took a deep breath. "It would be good to get away."

Simone was smiling. "I'll book the tickets and the rental car right now. Want me to research places to eat?"

"Nah. I can do that."

She turned to her computer, then paused. "Oh. Do you think you ought to run the travel plans by Dr. Tandy?"

He grimaced. "I probably should." He'd never traveled for FAE on business before. Here he was, Vice President of Global Operations, and he didn't even know if he had a travel budget. Denise controlled everything.

"I can ask her, if it's easier," Simone offered.

"No, no – I ought to talk to her about this new contact, anyway." He knew he was frowning. Denise didn't like it when he interrupted her during the day. She had made it clear, years before, that he was at *her* beck and call, not the other way around.

"I have a suggestion," Simone said. "Why not wait to talk to her 'til after we get back?"

He bit his lower lip, considering. "What's the advantage? Besides putting off an uncomfortable conversation, I mean."

She gave him a sly look. "Well, at this point you don't really know what's going on, right? You have to fly out there anyway. Just go out there and meet with them, and gather as much information as you can. Then you can give her a full report, instead of a lot of guesswork."

He looked at her with admiration. "You're good at this."

"Why, thank you." She tilted her head and smiled, then turned to the computer and hit a few keys. "Oh. There's a problem."

"Oh?"

"There's only one nonstop each day from San Francisco to Albuquerque. And there's only one nonstop for the return flight, too. How long is the drive?"

"Uh, I'm not sure. Maybe an hour and a half?" He pulled out his phone to verify it, but Simone was faster.

"You're right." She shook her head. "That's what I was afraid of. There isn't enough time to get to Los Alamos and back before the return flight leaves, let alone meet with the vendors."

"What about nonstops out of San Jose?"

She checked. "There aren't any at all."

"Well, then," he said, "I guess we'll have to stay overnight."

"You're the boss," she said with a broad smile.

New Mexico

Chapter 25

Jan arrived at work early, in case the courier arrived before the receptionist did. He didn't want to miss the delivery. The team was already twenty-four hours behind. Waiting for redelivery of the new specs would waste everybody's time.

But no courier arrived – early or later. By mid-morning, he was tired of twiddling his thumbs at his desk. He walked over to Bennie's office and poked his head in the open doorway. "Any word from FAE?"

"Didn't our good friend Mr. Jenkins copy you on his email?" Bennie said. He clicked the email open and sighed. "No, he did not." He turned to Jan. "He is making the trip himself, and flying commercial. However, the flight schedule is not very accommodating. He won't be here until late this afternoon."

"That's just great," Jan groused. "I got up at the crack of dawn to make sure I didn't miss the guy. I could have slept in."

"I apologize," Bennie said. "I should have made sure you were on the email chain."

Jan waved him off. "I'm the one who should be apologizing. I shouldn't have taken my frustration out on you."

"No worries. I feel the same way. This guy is really yanking us around."

"I hope this contract is worth it," Jan said.

"So do I," Bennie said. "When he gets here, I will let you know. I'm sure he will have the front desk contact me. But I want you to be the one to escort him around."

"Of course," Jan said. "Guess I'll go find some busywork for the next several hours."

Jan went back to his desk and shut the door. Then he sat in his guest chair and stared out the window.

He pondered whether to try to contact the kid now, but he didn't know his schedule or his habits. Jenkins would have to be in a situation where his defenses were down – say, if he were sleeping on the plane. But Jan had no way of knowing whether he was, and he didn't want to risk tipping his hand to find out.

He sighed and stretched his legs out under his desk. He could use a nap himself, but he didn't want to risk allowing himself to be vulnerable to the same sort of intrusion. That's how Jenkins had gotten inside his defenses the last time.

Instead, he tried tapping into his Sight.

He would never be as good at calling it up as Tandy had wanted him to be. But he had made progress at the Institute – no thanks to her abusive tactics – and he'd been able to refine his skill further in the decades since breaking free of the place. He might not be able to count on it coming when he called, but he knew how to create the conditions to encourage it to manifest.

So he stared out the window at the parking lot, unfocused his eyes, and eased his senses open.

Slowly, foreknowledge came to him. And part of it surprised him.

Oh, Tandy's M.O. hadn't changed. She was still on the lookout for talented kids she could exploit, but she seemed more cautious now. Maybe her age played a part – or maybe it was something else. He had the sense she was looking over her shoulder, as if her past might catch up with her.

Well, it would, if he and Janis had their way. He didn't get the sense that she was on the lookout for them, though. So maybe something else was scaring her. He'd have to ask Janis to take a look.

He shifted his attention to the kid who was on his way here. Jenkins's talent definitely had a bait-and-switch flavor; Jan's company wasn't his first victim. And he could See for sure now that FAE had never planned any sort of project or experiment for the Mars mission. It was all about having access to NASA's communications infrastructure, so

168

that Jenkins could use it to boost his signal and find more people like him – people with talent that Tandy could exploit.

But if Jenkins' recruitment effort paid off, Jan could See, he would never be anything more than a lackey in Tandy's talent army. She had given him a fancy title, but she was also playing on his fear of being abandoned – an angle she had played with both Janis and Jan, once upon a time.

There was no way out for Jenkins; he was in too deep with her. She would use him until he was used up. Then she would discard him and pounce on the most promising candidate he had recruited for her. But…

Jan was shocked. He could clearly see another timeline running alongside the current one. That had never happened to him before.

Usually what he Saw were variations on a theme – multiple chains of events with slight variances in timing or execution, but with every chain coming together and resolving the same way in the end. Choices had consequences, after all, and someone who made Choice A in one situation would likely make Choice A every time they were presented with a similar situation. That habit or tendency was what made some people believe their fate was sealed, or that it had been determined before they were born. But everybody was always free to break the mold and make a different choice. They just didn't. The rut they were in felt too comfortable. Or someone had convinced them – or they had convinced themselves – that they had no other choice.

For whatever reason, Jenkins felt Tandy had him backed into a corner. And when someone like him ran up against a sociopath like her, you didn't need a talent for Seeing the future to know where it would lead.

Except there was this other concurrent timeline to one side, and it appeared it was aiming to intersect with the one Jenkins was on. And that collision could throw everything off-course. Jenkins could still be saved, after all, and Tandy could be brought to justice.

Jan was pretty sure he and Janis weren't the wild card riding this other timeline. But they could definitely help it along.

The phone on his desk rang, jolting him out of his reverie. Awkwardly, he reached around his laptop and snagged the phone from its cradle before the third ring. "Marek," he said by way of greeting.

"They're stopping for lunch," Bennie complained. "And *shopping*. It will be the end of the day before they get here."

"Who's 'they'? I thought Jenkins was coming alone."

"A last-minute addition to his team," Bennie said. "That's what he said, at least. I have no idea what's going on."

"And that's just the way he likes it," Jan muttered.

"I didn't hear you."

"Sorry. I was talking to myself." He glanced at his cellphone for the time, then thought for a moment. "Yeah. I can stay."

"I wouldn't normally ask you, especially as you came in so early ..." Bennie began.

"No, I get it, really. It's fine. The situation is fluid. I had planned to visit a friend tonight, but I can call and let her know."

"Her?" Bennie said. "I thought you were gay."

"And I didn't think you listened to office gossip," Jan said, teasing him.

"Oh, I listen to it. I just don't always understand it."

"Right. Because your English is so poor."

"My Engrish not so poor. Long time no understand American humor," Bennie said. Jan could hear the grin in his voice.

"Okay, Jackie Chan," he said. "If you need to head home, go on. I can sit in the lobby and wait for these jokers after Franca leaves for the day."

"That would be great," Bennie said, relief evident in his voice.

Jan's Sight kicked in. Bennie's wife was pregnant with twins. Her doctor had some concerns about her health right now, but Jan knew the babies would arrive safely and would grow like weeds. "Sure," he said. "No problem. I'll let you know tomorrow morning how it goes."

"Perfect. Talk to you tomorrow."

Jan reached around the laptop to put the phone in its cradle. Then he used his cell phone to call Janis. "Hi," he said. "Can you talk?"

"Sure. I'm on my way home. How's our Mr. Jenkins?"

Jan blew out a breath. "He's not here yet. He and his colleague decided to stop on the way here for lunch and shopping."

"Shopping? Really? Who's this colleague?"

"No idea. Listen, could you do me a favor?"

"Of course. Anything."

That made him smile. "It's nothing too nefarious," he assured her. "It's just that I had a little episode earlier today."

"Oh?"

"I think our mutual friend is scared of something. Could you check into that?"

She sounded doubtful. "I can try. But I've never had much luck with that avenue of inquiry before."

"I know, I know. Sorry to ask you to try it again." He paused. "Maybe you could run at the problem obliquely. Like you did that other time. You know."

"Hmm. Possibly. I'll let you know how I get on."

"Sounds good. I'll give you a ring when I'm done with the kid and his colleague, if it's not too late."

"Feel free to call anytime," she said. "This might take me a while to suss out."

Chapter 26

"Well, he doesn't ask for much, does he?" Janis groused to herself. "First he can't tell me when he'll be done tonight, and then he expects me to do a deep-dive into that woman's past. Just like that!"

She wasn't really angry at Jan — just blowing off steam. She wanted to be in a calm state of mind before trying to look into Tandy's past. She knew it was probably going to be an exercise in frustration, and she wanted to be on her game before she even began to try.

So she did not rush getting home. Then she made herself dinner, ate it, and cleaned up the kitchen. She even poured herself a glass of wine, in case the alcohol might help her to relax. At this stage of her life, it was more likely to put her to sleep, but she thought it was worth a try.

She knew her reluctance was due to performance anxiety. Other than the first time she'd met Tandy, she'd never had any luck with diving into what made her tick. Psychologically, the woman was easy to read; she gave every outward sign of being a psychopath. But it was her interior life Janis was interested in. That could go a long way in explaining what turned someone into a monster.

She had no desire to make excuses for Tandy, or let her off the hook in any way. The woman had ordered her sterilized for no medical reason; she simply wanted to make sure she and Jan didn't gang up against her. Janis had had to live with the consequences of Tandy's choices for virtually all of her life. They had profoundly impacted decisions she herself had made as an adult. No, Tandy deserved neither understanding nor forgiveness.

But that back story was important to know if she and Jan were to be successful in seeing justice served, at long last. So while she was annoyed that Jan had asked her to look into Tandy's past *again*, she was also glad to have an excuse to give it another try.

The only time she had ever gotten it to work before was by reading the past of someone tangentially related to Tandy. In her successful previous attempt, she'd used Mr. Carruthers. She supposed she could use him again. The other obvious choice was Antoine Jenkins, but all she had to go on there was his photo on the FAE website and his questionable biography. Janis didn't know enough about him to find a way in.

So. Carruthers. She sipped her wine, then pulled out a copy of the article in the fraternity magazine and studied it.

In her mind's eye, she could see the room where the interview took place – Carruthers' office. Not the one at the Institute, because that had been long gone by the time this interview had taken place. And anyway, this one was much nicer – thick carpet and lots of mahogany. The interview must have occurred when he was working for the company that had been shut down for fraud. The one Tandy had plugged too hard on that podcast. Carruthers had done a stint in prison for it, but Tandy apparently hadn't.

It seemed like as good a place as any to start.

She followed the thread of Carruthers' past … and there was Tandy, pestering him about giving her a job. She wasn't as young as she had been at the Institute, making two kids' lives a living hell, but she was still fairly young and attractive. He didn't seem all that excited about hiring her, though. "Why would I hire a liar?" he told her coldly.

So by then the affair must have been over. Maybe he'd even figured out that she didn't have any paranormal talent. Why *would* he hire a liar?

"Because I know things about the way you do business," she told him evenly. "Things that could get you into serious trouble."

He hemmed and hawed for a little while longer, but he did eventually hire her, as evidenced by her appearance on that podcast.

Carruthers didn't interest her anymore, so she made a jump sideways to Tandy's life.

Her early years were as shrouded from Janis as they had always been. But she had more experience with her talent now, and more life experience in general, to figure out why she could get only so far and no farther: It was because Tandy herself had blocked off access to those years. She had seen the same sort of reaction in traumatized high schoolers who came through her library – they had slammed up a mental block to keep the memories of their trauma from hurting them any further.

Tandy's early years must have been horrific for that block to have held for so long.

It hit Janis that this had been her problem all along. Every time previously that she had tried to access Tandy's past, she had been looking for those early memories. She had wanted to know what made Tandy the horrible human being she had become. But the events that explained it were behind Tandy's mental barrier. She couldn't get into Tandy's history because she couldn't get past the wall.

She was still interested in that, of course, but she and Jan had a more immediate problem. And Tandy's memories that related to *that* were much more accessible.

So she went back as far as she could, up to the point where she and Jan had left the Institute. Their departure had created a whole lot of headaches for the woman – more than eighteen-year-old Janis could ever have envisioned, but that made perfect sense to sixty-year-old Janis. Tandy and Carruthers tried to save face by simply shutting the Institute down, but their investors – some of whom had been along since its inception, nearly twenty years before – had not been happy. They wanted a return on their investment or they wanted their money back. And of course, there was no money to give back – Tandy and Carruthers had spent it all, on the building, the staff, the kids, and the lavish salaries they paid themselves.

So for the next ten years or so, Tandy's life was consumed by one lawsuit after another – first on charges of fraud and unjust enrichment, and then, when those judgments went against her, more lawsuits when she didn't pay the court-ordered restitution. No wonder she had begged Carruthers for a job. Her legal troubles had left her flat broke.

And yes, he had dumped her and gone back to his wife after the Institute closed down. They resumed the affair briefly – just long enough, it seemed, for Tandy to convince Carruthers to deed the Institute property over to her. Then Carruthers' new house of cards collapsed. This time, though, Tandy was too low on the totem pole to share in Carruthers' legal troubles. So he went to prison and she …

Well. She traveled to Central America, where she got involved in, and then took over, a child prostitution ring (which seemed in character for her to Janis). That got the attention of the head of the local drug cartel. El Serpiente made her his mistress. She even convinced him to pay for her plastic surgery.

When the authorities busted his operation, she escaped again – back to California, where she moved into the former home of the Institute and rebranded it as FAE. This time, she was a lot smarter about how to run a successful scam, and when Antoine landed on her doorstep, she groomed him more skillfully than she had groomed Jan and her.

There had never been any intention to put talents on Mars. What Tandy was after was a way to find more people to make money for her. She thought of it as her retirement plan – an income in perpetuity, all by having a few kids under her control.

Janis sat back, revolted. Not even the wine she was drinking could wash away the bad taste this woman's life had left in her mouth.

"And to think we both went into fields involving children," she muttered. The difference, she knew, was that her own intention had always been to help the kids she came in contact with – and she was driven to it because she couldn't have children of her own. Tandy, on the other hand, saw children only as malleable little creatures to exploit.

She had only seen a tiny bit of Antoine's story – not enough, perhaps, to discover much about him – but she gave it a try anyway. The result was only a little helpful. It appeared Antoine came to the Institute

– sorry, to FAE – via an acquaintance who knew his parents. The boy lied so convincingly, creating unreal scenarios that people actually believed had happened to them, that his parents were at their wit's end. He was about ten when Tandy got her clutches into him.

Not much older than Jan had been, Janis realized. That seemed like a thing he ought to know.

She glanced at the clock and started. She had been at this for hours, and still there had been no word from him. Her earlier aggravation turned to outright worry. She texted him:

Are you still with him? She got him at about age 10, if that helps.

She sat back, steeling herself for a long wait. But his response came within the next few minutes:

Very interesting. Thanks! Talk to you soon.

"Well, isn't that cryptic," she said, and downed the last of her wine.

Chapter 27

Jan's belly growled long before Antoine arrived. He ordered a pizza, then went out to the reception area to wait for the delivery guy. He figured if he was still eating it when Antoine and his colleague showed up, they could wait for him to finish. He'd waited hours for them.

The receptionist had already gone for the day. He settled in at her desk, where the button to unlock the front door was easily accessible. He was tempted to raise the seat of her chair to accommodate his much longer legs, but he didn't want to be a jerk about it.

Dan passed him on his way out to the parking lot. He put his hands on his hips. "Got yourself a promotion, I see."

Jan grinned. "Just temporary."

"You still waiting around for that client of ours?"

"Yeah. Oh, here's my dinner." Jan buzzed the delivery guy in, signed the credit card slip, and let the guy back out.

"Be sure to submit that for reimbursement," Dan said. "Don't bother Bennie with it – bring it straight to me."

"Thanks," said Jan. "I'm always happy to have the company buy me a meal."

Dan laughed. "*We're* not paying for it. It's going on FAE's bill. By the way." He approached the desk and leaned over to speak more quietly. "I made a few phone calls today on this outfit. You know they claim to have a guy from NASA on their board of directors?"

"I'll take your word for it," said Jan.

"Okay. Anyway, our contact at NASA says there's no one at the agency by that name. It's not even a legit job title."

"Huh. Next you're gonna tell me they're not devoted to excellence, like their company name says. Okay with you if I ...?" he said, pointing to his pizza.

"Sure, sure. Just don't leave a mess on Franca's desk or I'll never hear the end of it."

Jan drew an X in the air over the center of his chest and dug in.

"Man, that smells good. You're making me hungry," Dan said. "I'm outta here."

Jan chewed and swallowed. "You don't want to stay and meet these jokers?"

"Are you kidding? I put you in charge so I wouldn't have to."

"Final offer," Jan said, and took another bite.

Dan waved and headed out the door.

Jan had time to finish his dinner, meticulously wipe down Franca's desk, and dump his trash in the break room. He was just beginning to think about starting the voucher for his meal receipt when a couple of smartly-dressed young people approached the door. The young man made a gallant move to open the glass door for the woman, but the locked door checked his swing. The look on his face was so comical that Jan almost burst into laughter. He took a moment to school his features into inscrutability, then hit the buzzer and strode out from behind Franca's desk to greet them.

"I'm Jan Marek. You must be Antoine Jenkins," Jan said, holding out his hand to the couple.

"I am," said Jenkins, "and this is my … associate, Simone."

"Simone Brown," she said.

She had put out her hand as soon as Jan did, so he shook hers first, then his. "Nice to meet you both. This way, please." He led them around the corner to the company's smaller conference room. "I'm afraid all I have to offer you is bottled water. The staff usually has the coffee pot going, but they have already gone home for the day."

"Yes, well, we're very sorry we're so late," Antoine said. "We had some trouble with the car rental at the airport, and then lunch took a lot longer than we expected."

178

"And the hotel wouldn't let us check in until four," Simone explained.

"Hotel?" Jan asked. "Where are you staying?"

"It's in Santa Fe, right on the plaza," Simone said.

"An excellent choice. Santa Fe is a wonderful city," he said. "Much more picturesque than Los Alamos."

"I just love the architecture," she said, practically simpering.

"Yes, well, in any case," said Antoine, frowning at her, "we don't need any refreshments."

"Oh! No, I'm good," Simone said, smiling broadly at both of them.

"All right," said Jan. "In that case, please have a seat and we'll get started."

"Sounds good," said Antoine, sitting in the chair to the right of the head of the table. "I think we can wrap this up fairly quickly."

Simone sat across from him and folded her hands atop the table. Jan took the seat on the end, between them. "I'm sure we can," he said as he scooted in his chair. "You do have the new specs with you?"

"Of course," said Antoine, and handed him a hard drive.

Jan weighed it in one hand. "You don't happen to have a printout, do you?"

"Well, no," Antoine said. "It's a fairly long document. We're trying to save trees and all that. Plus the weight of carrying it on the plane."

"Sure, of course," Jan said. He pulled his laptop out of the briefcase he had brought with him and fired it up, then plugged the drive into the USB port. He glanced up at his guests. "I just want to take a quick look at it before you go, if that's okay."

Antoine spread his hands wide. "Of course. Why wouldn't it be okay?" But Jan caught him shift his eyes sideways at Simone.

Jan had decided to test Bennie's theory that Jenkins saw him as an authority figure, and an out-of-date one, to boot, by playing the geezer. He took his time going over the files on the hard drive and made sure to wear a frown, as if all this newfangled technology was beyond him.

179

"Can I help you with accessing the data?" Jenkins offered. "It should have come right up."

It had, but Jenkins couldn't see his screen. "Just a minute," Jan muttered, clicking the trackpad on nothing several times. "Ah!" he said triumphantly, and beamed at the young people. "Here we go." He bent to study his screen, scrolling through the content. Then he muttered to himself and fished around in his briefcase for a pair of glasses he never wore. He put them on, scrolled a bit more, and then sat back with a sigh.

"Something wrong?" Jenkins asked.

"Well," Jan said with a laugh, "I don't know." He took off the glasses and laid them on the table next to the computer. "Maybe you brought the wrong hard drive. I don't see anything in any of these specs about Project Terraform."

"Right, no, there won't be," Jenkins said. "We've dropped that part of our proposal."

"Mr. Jenkins," he said, "there's no proposal involved. We're not hiring *you* – *you* hired *us*. To help you with a project for NASA related to their manned mission to Mars. That's what we signed on to do for you. If you're saying the Mars mission is no longer the focus of the work you want us to do, we need to renegotiate the contract. For our mutual protection."

Jenkins glanced at Simone helplessly. She said, "How long will that take?"

"To draw up a new contract?" Jan shrugged. "I couldn't say. That's not my area of expertise. But under the circumstances, I would expect we'd have to get our lawyers involved."

"What?" Jenkins spluttered. "But that's preposterous! That will take days! We don't have that kind of time!"

"You're right – we *don't* have that kind of time," Jan said. "Our team has already spun its wheels for two days, waiting for these new specs." He gestured at the hard drive. "Now we will have to spend additional time retooling for your new focus, which is …" He made a show of putting the readers back on and peering at the screen again. "Well," he said with a sigh, "it's a little hard to tell. But it sure looks to me like you want us to build you a back door into NASA's communications infrastructure."

"I wouldn't phrase it quite that way," Jenkins said.

"Oh? How would you phrase it, then?"

Jenkins threw another mute appeal to Simone. She grimaced and shook her head.

"All right, then, Mr. Jenkins. Maybe you could answer another question for me." Jan reached again into his briefcase and brought out the hard copy Janis had given him of the FAE webpage listing their board of directors. He slid it toward Jenkins and pointed at a name. "This gentleman here. The one who works for NASA."

"What about him?" Jenkins asked warily.

"He doesn't," Jan said simply. "We've checked with our contact at NASA. There's no one there by that name and no title like his in the whole organization. Moreover," he said, embroidering on what Dan had told him, "they've never heard of FAE. Now how could that be, when you told us you needed our help on your contract with them?"

"That's not so!" Jenkins said hotly.

And suddenly Jan knew he was wrong. Everything he'd just said was wrong. The guy from NASA on FAE's board did exist – their contact must have just overlooked him in the staff directory. And FAE did have a contract with NASA, an ongoing one, involving …

Jan chuckled, dispelling the fantasy. "You're good, Mr. Jenkins," he said. "You're very good. You've had me going twice now. First with the FAE base on Mars to contact extraterrestrials, and now this."

Jenkins's mouth dropped open. "You're the guy," he said. "You're the talent." He leaned forward, his eyes wide. "Look, Mr. Marek, we would love to have you on our team. We *need* you. I've never met *anyone* who can shut me out like you can."

Jan's cell phone chirped. He pulled it out of his pocket and glanced at it. "Pardon me," he said. "I've got to attend to this." He read Janis's text and gears dropped into place in his head. *Antoine, you poor bastard. I was you, forty years ago.* He fired off a reply, typing rapidly with both thumbs, and looked up to see the young folks staring at him. *Oh, right. I guess I should have put the readers back on and fumbled with the technology. Well, it's too late now — the cat's out of the bag.*

He considered his next words carefully. "Son," he said, "I've been on your team. I got out. And I'd like to help you do the same."

"I ... I don't ..." Jenkins stammered. His eyes flew to Simone's face.

Jan looked to her, too. Her features radiated compassion – and something else. "I'll help, too," she said quietly. All of her earlier ditziness was gone.

Jan realized he was looking at the concurrent timeline he'd Seen that afternoon, and smiled.

Jenkins stood. "I think we're done here," he said, his voice unsteady. "I need to talk this over with my boss and find out how she wants us to proceed."

"That's fair," Jan said. "I'll walk you to the door." He pulled his wallet from his back pocket, flipped it open, and extracted one of his business cards, which he offered to Jenkins. "You'll still be in the area in the morning, right? Give me a call and let me know how you plan to proceed."

Jenkins nodded and took it. He looked lost.

Jan waved them through the conference room door and out to the lobby. He hit the button next to the front door to unlock it, then held it open for them. "Please give Dr. Tandy my regards," Jan said to Jenkins as he passed. The man's eyes flew to his, then looked away again. He nearly ran to his rental car.

Simone hung back. "Thank you," she said.

"Is he sleeping with her?" Jan asked.

Simone nodded tightly and looked down.

Jan sighed. "Nothing ever changes. How do I contact you?"

"I'll be in touch," she said, and followed Jenkins to the car.

Jan watched them go. Once he was certain they were on the road, he went back to the conference room to collect his gear.

He called Janis on his own way home. "Thanks for your text," he told her. "It was quite timely."

"Oh, good," she said. "It seemed to me it would be helpful for you to know that."

Her voice had an odd cadence, as if she were trying to enunciate very carefully. "Are you drunk?" he asked with a grin.

"I wouldn't say *drunk* exactly," she said. "Maybe a little tipsy."

"Right. How much of the bottle did you drink?"

"I didn't finish it!" she said, which made him laugh quite loudly indeed. "You took a very long time to get back to me," she continued. "I had to do *some*thing to fill my time."

"If only I weren't so old and tired," he said, "I'd come over and take advantage of you."

"You cad," she said delightedly. "We'll just have to do it another time."

"It's a date," he said.

Chapter 28

The drive from Los Alamos to the hotel in Santa Fe took less than an hour. Antoine spent all of it thinking furiously about how to tell Denise what had just transpired.

"Just tell her," Simone said, breaking the silence.

"Easy for you to say," he returned. He didn't even ask how she knew what he was thinking. It seemed obvious to him. What else would he be thinking about?

"I mean it," she said. "Just tell her the truth. Don't embroider it, or try to get her to see some alternate version of events."

He took his eyes off the road for a moment to stare at her.

"What? You think I didn't know?" she said. "You think I never knew when you tried it on me?" She shook his head. "You have a lot to learn, Antoine."

"Yeah? Like what?"

"Like there's a life outside of FAE," she said. "Like it wouldn't be the end of the world if you quit."

"Can't quit," he mumbled. "No good for anything else."

"That's *her* talking," Simone said.

He stopped listening. Denise was good for him. He had to stay. He had nowhere else to go.

Simone had reserved two hotel rooms – one for each of them. Antoine had been a little disappointed when he first found out, but now he was glad. He didn't want to call Denise with her listening to every word. She was already all up in his business.

Once behind his own closed door, he debated with himself. Should he call her now or in the morning? He could call her office number and leave her a voicemail, but that seemed like the coward's way out. It was awfully late to call now, though – she'd be at home, maybe getting ready for bed. Maybe already in bed. Maybe already in bed with someone who wasn't him.

That didn't bear thinking about.

Then he remembered California was in a different time zone. It was an hour earlier there. She never went to bed this early.

If he waited 'til morning, his nerves wouldn't let him sleep. But if he called her now, the bitching out she was likely to give him would probably keep him up, anyway.

"Man up, Jenkins," he muttered, and dialed her number.

She answered on the first ring. "Where the hell are you?" she demanded.

"Uh …"

"I've been looking for you all day!" she went on at the same volume. "I went to your office this morning and it was dark. That secretary of yours wasn't in, either. Did you give her the day off? Did I *authorize* you to give her the day off?"

"N-no, Denise …"

"You may call me Dr. Tandy," she said icily.

"Yes, Dr. Tandy."

"That's better. Now, I repeat: Where the hell are you?"

"In New Mexico," he answered miserably.

"New Mexico? What for?"

"See," he began, "we needed to deliver a new set of specs to the Project Terraform vendor …"

"You couldn't use FedEx?" she demanded.

"I felt more comfortable delivering them myself," he said, gathering a semblance of his usual self-assurance. "Given the delicate nature of the information."

"I suppose that makes sense," she said grudgingly. "So you hand delivered the package this afternoon."

"Yes," he hedged. Taking the time difference into account, calling it *this afternoon* wasn't exactly lying.

"And what did they say?"

He took a deep breath. "They want to renegotiate the contract."

"WHAT?"

"Because our project isn't really part of Terraform anymore," he explained. "Our contact told me it would be better to draw up a new contract – one that actually reflects the scope of the project we're hiring them to do."

"Who is this contact of yours?" she said. "I need to call him. This is bullshit."

Antoine pulled the man's card out of the pocket of his blazer. "Jan Marek," he read aloud.

The line seemed to go dead.

"Dr. Tandy?" Antoine asked. "Are you still there?"

Her voice faltered. "What did you say his name was?"

"Jan Marek. He said I should give you his regards. Do you want his number?"

"No," she said, regaining her usual self-assurance. "Stay put. I'm coming out there."

California, 1978

Chapter 29

The night before Jan turned eighteen, he reached his breaking point.

He had avoided Tandy since the attack – he could not bear to call it what it really had been – by simply not showing up for his scheduled training sessions. He expected, every waking moment, to be summoned to her office to explain his insubordination, but the summons never came.

That should have eased his anxiety over time – but the lack of communication from her also meant he had no idea what her plans for him were, once he became an adult.

"Has she talked to you?" he asked Janis at one point.

"Not at all," she said. She had stopped going to her training sessions, too. She said it was in solidarity, but Jan knew she had as little desire to see Tandy as he did.

"So she's just going to leave us hanging?" he said.

Janis shrugged. "Apparently."

"You know, you're awfully blasé about this." His hands closed into fists at his sides. "Don't you care about getting out of here?"

Her mouth dropped open. "What are you getting mad at *me* for? You know I care! We're in this together, remember?"

"It's just that sometimes it doesn't feel like it," he muttered, and turned to walk away.

"Jan," she called, her voice gentler. He stopped, but didn't turn back to her. "Look. I know this is making you nuts. It's making *me* nuts, too. But I think …" She paused. "I think from her point of view, this is a perfect setup. If we're not talking to each other, we can't gang up against *her*. Right?"

His shoulders slumped.

"She has us right where she wants us," she said bitterly. "Now she can let our birthdays pass as if they're just another day."

He turned back to her. "But when we're adults, we can walk out those doors." He pointed toward where he thought the front of the building might be.

"Right, I know. But there's a security guard. And beyond that, there's a gate. *Some*body has to let us *out*, Jan."

"The guard will have to do it," he said. "He'll *have* to."

"Okay," she said. "So we're out. Where do we go?"

"I can contact my parents," he said.

"How? Do you know their phone number?" She only paused for a second – she knew the answer. "Of course you don't. But Tandy does."

"She holds all the cards," he said bitterly. "We're never getting out of here."

"Oh, we're getting out," she said. "But we need to have a plan. And we can't come up with one if we're always arguing."

"Fine," he snapped. "You think of a plan and let me know." He went to his room and slammed the door.

If Janis had ever come up with a workable plan, she never shared it with him. And with each passing day, his sense of failure grew.

The night before his birthday, he couldn't take it anymore. He lay awake, tossing and turning, trying to come up with some way to gain his release. The only plan that seemed even remotely viable was to let himself into Tandy's office, find his parents' phone number, and call them to come and get him. But what if her office door was locked? What if she was still there, having sex with somebody on that damned loveseat of hers? What if he ran into her and she attacked him again?

His brain was a jumble of fear and hopelessness, but at last he threw himself out of bed and got dressed. Then he let himself out of his room, closing his door, and moved as silently past the lounge as he could.

Janis's door was closed and no light showed at the bottom of the door. He hesitated for a moment, thinking maybe he should knock. Let her know where he was going. Ask her if she wanted to come along. She had said they were in this together, after all.

But his misery wouldn't allow him her company. He glided on.

The door of their quarters creaked when he opened it, and the locking mechanism *clicked* louder in the stillness than it ever had before. He paused, his heart in his mouth, waiting for a sleepy Janis to yank her own door open and demand to know what he was up to. But she didn't. He let out the breath he'd been holding and went on his way.

As he rounded the corner of the hallway where Tandy's office was located, he froze. Her door was wide open and the light was on, spilling out into the hallway. He heard voices. One was hers; the other was male.

He sank down onto the carpet and sat with his back to the wall, elbows braced on knees and his head in his hands. His plan wasn't going to work. It never had any chance of working. She was always, always, *always* there. Lurking. Leering. Wrecking his life.

He couldn't stay there. There was no telling how long it would take before they were done. So he levered himself up and went walking through the halls and stairwells of the Institute.

He found himself, at last, at the top of a side stairwell. There was only one way out – a door labeled, *ROOF*. He pulled it open, expecting an alarm to go off, but none did.

The roof was not an exciting place to be. It was flat, with a low wall of pale bricks as its perimeter. The bricks glowed a bit in the moonlight. The material underfoot was some kind of pebbled paper. There were metal shafts and odd bits of pipe sticking up here and there.

The door he had just emerged from closed with a *clang*. Startled, he turned around. He tried the knob; it turned easily in his hand. He let out a breath. He wasn't stuck out here, at least. Unless he wanted to be.

He looked up, dazzled. He and Janis spent nearly all of their time indoors, and the few times they had been allowed out onto the grounds, it had always been daylight. Nothing in his experience prepared him for the full width and breadth of a cloudless, moonlit sky. He had read about

191

stars, but he had no idea there were so many of them. Even the security lights atop the wall that surrounded the Institute couldn't significantly dim their brilliance.

That wall. Jan tore his eyes away from the canopy of stars and studied it. He couldn't see the front gate from here – only the edge of the parking lot and an ancillary building or two. But the wall surrounded everything. And it looked high. Not as high as the roof he was standing on, but certainly too high to climb.

Janis was right. They would have to leave through the front gate, and Tandy held the key.

She would never let them go.

He took a seat on the brick wall, then swiveled on his butt until his legs dangled over the drop. He looked as far over the edge as he dared. The building here was three stories tall, not two, as he'd always thought. Would it be enough?

He stood and balanced himself on the top of the wall. He thought of Janis and what he was leaving her to face alone. He loved her. He knew this would hurt her. But he couldn't bear to continue living in limbo.

He slid one foot forward. His toes dangled over the edge.

"Jan!" screamed Janis from the doorway.

He turned too fast, throwing off his center of balance. He flailed comically, then cartwheeled into space.

She hadn't been asleep when he left. She'd been trying desperately to find a way into Tandy's past. As usual, it didn't work.

Then something prompted her to slide sideways into Jan's history. His recent history. And there she found the source of his pain – the thing he couldn't bring himself to share with anyone. Not even her.

Horrified, she dropped out of the memory stream and came back to herself. That was when she realized she had heard him leave. She got up and checked; he was still gone.

She got dressed quickly and headed out, not caring how much noise she made.

Anger sent her first to Tandy's office, but the light was out and the door was locked. He couldn't be in there.

She knew he sometimes rambled around the building. He could be anywhere. She closed her eyes and let her sense of him guide her – up three floors to the door to the roof.

His surprise at hearing her call his name was genuine. But he was too far off-balance to catch himself, and she couldn't reach him in time.

She ran to the edge and looked over. He lay sprawled on the grass below. She screamed his name again, then turned and ran back through the door to the stairwell.

She had no memory, later, of her headlong flight down the stairs, other than hoping she didn't trip and end up in a heap. Her next clear memory was of bursting into the lobby, startling the security guard out of his nap, and demanding, "Call an ambulance! Jan fell off the roof!" Then she shoved her way through the door – the guard buzzed it open for her, thankfully – and ran to where her friend lay.

He hadn't moved, but he was breathing. It was only then that she allowed herself to burst into tears.

Jan came to gradually. He pried his eyes open and groaned. He could tell he wasn't in his room at the Institute, and he doubted this too-bright room, with its medical equipment in a corner and a bag of clear liquid feeding a needle taped to his hand, was the afterlife.

"Hi," Janis said.

"Hi," he said. "I guess I survived."

She blushed. "I'm sorry," she whispered. "I think I made you fall when I yelled."

"No, don't. Don't apologize. It wasn't your fault. I had every intention of handling it myself." He tried to scoot up in the bed, but realized he was stuck in position – his left leg wore a cast and was

193

elevated in a sling. His left hand was in a cast, too, nearly up to the elbow.

"Don't move," she said belatedly.

He barked a laugh. "Thanks," he said. "So how much damage did I do?"

Janis's eyes slid to the door. Jan followed her look, and realized for the first time that someone else was in the room with them – a brown-haired young man with a bushy red mustache. "Jake?" he said.

The man grinned. "I didn't think you'd remember me. Hiya, Champ."

"How could I forget you?" Jan said. "I never heard anybody else go up against Tandy the way you did. Uh … Champ?"

"Hey, you did what you set out to do. You got the two of you out of that hellhole. That makes you a champ in my book."

Jan closed his eyes and relaxed his neck so that his head fell back onto the pillow. "I meant to die," he said.

He heard Jake approach the bed, then felt the man grip the shoulder that wasn't sore. He opened his eyes. "You *meant* to get out of there by any means necessary," Jake said. "And it worked. You're here. You had to shatter your heel and break your wrist in three or four places, but you're out. And so is she."

Janis came to his side and stroked his bangs back from his forehead. "I wish you'd told me what she did to you," she said.

"Oh, God," he groaned, turning away. "You Saw."

"And then she told me," Jake said. "And I'm glad she did. Sexual abuse of a minor is a *crime*, Champ. That bitch could do time for what she did."

Jan turned back. "Really?"

"You bet your ass, really." He and Janis exchanged a glance. "And that gave me the leverage I needed with Uncle Ray."

"We're not going back, Jan," said Janis with a big-eyed smile. "Either one of us."

"How?" Jan managed.

"When the security guard called Uncle Ray's house to notify him of your accident, I happened to pick up the phone. My uncle had already turned in for the night, so I met the ambulance here. When I got the skinny from Janis" – here he nodded at her – "I had a long talk with my uncle. He agreed it was in everybody's best interest that I manage affairs for the two of you from here on out."

"He's getting us an apartment," Janis said. "He says we'll have to learn how to cook and clean, though."

"Sounds like a fair trade," Jan said. "What about our stuff?"

"All taken care of," said Jake. "I'm hiring movers to pack you guys up and move everything to your new place. And Uncle Ray is arranging for high school diplomas for you both. You'll still have to take placement tests and so on if you decide to go to college, but the Institute will pay for them. *And* for your college tuition." Jake grinned and stepped back. "All *you* have to do, my man, is get well. The doc said you'll need surgery on that heel, and maybe on the wrist, too. He'll know more once the swelling goes down."

Jan felt like crying. A huge weight had lifted off his shoulders. For the first time in his life, it seemed, he felt hopeful. "Why are you doing this?" he asked. "I mean, thank you, but why?"

Jake laughed. "I have seen some ugly things in my life, Champ, but the scam that bitch has been running on you two is the ugliest thing I've *ever* seen. I had to make it right, that's all." He winked and gave Jan a lazy salute. "I'll be back by before the docs let you go. Coming?" He directed the last word at Janis.

"Can you wait for me?" she said.

"Sure. I'll be down in the lobby." He nodded at her and let himself out.

The two of them gazed at each other. "I'm sorry," Jan croaked.

"For what?"

"I knew if I died, it would hurt you. But I couldn't …"

She put a finger to his lips. "Shh. I've hidden something from you, too."

"What?" He couldn't imagine her hiding any secret as unspeakable as his.

She carefully took his hand with the needle stuck in the back and laced her fingers through his. "You know when Tandy had my tubes tied?"

"Yeah?"

"You know what the worst part of it was? Once I got past feeling helpless and violated, I mean."

"No. What?"

She laughed a little. "I didn't realize until then that I'd wanted to have your child." He could see tears in her eyes. "I knew we'd be together forever, and once we got out of there, everything would be perfect. We'd get married and have kids and be a real family. But we can't."

His damned Sight chose that moment to kick in and show him his future – and hers. When he came back to himself, he was crying. "Janis," he said. "It was never going to be that way."

"What? What do you mean?"

"You and I ..." He tried wiping his wet cheek on his pillow. "You and I are going to be going our separate ways. We have different paths ahead of us. And it's going to be best that we not ... contact each other."

Her lower lip trembled. "But why?"

He sniffed. "It seems like we'll be safe enough if we don't call attention to ourselves. But if we stick together, it will be too easy for Tandy to get at us again. So as soon as we can, we need to split up. No contact with Jake or his uncle. And if that doesn't work..." He sniffed again. "If Tandy somehow finds one of us, at least she won't find both of us."

"You Saw all this?"

196

"Just now." He sucked in a ragged breath. "But someday, a long time from now, we'll see each other again."

"When?"

He shook his head. "Years from now. There's a young guy involved. That's all I know. But when he shows up, I'll come and find you."

"But I love you," she said, and kissed the back of his hand.

He kissed her hair. "I love you, too. I wish it could be different."

"Maybe you're wrong," she said. But they both knew he was never wrong about the future.

New Mexico

Chapter 30

Janis's phone rang early the following morning. "How's your head?" Jan asked.

"Ugh. You horrible man," she said, which elicited a hearty laugh from him. "It's fine, thank you very much. I didn't have *that* much to drink."

"Good," he said, "because I think the two of us may need a liquid lunch today."

"Oh?"

"I just got off the phone with the kid. He had a less than productive conversation with our mutual friend last night. She arrives in Albuquerque early this afternoon."

"She's coming *here*?" Janis squeaked. "Oh, dear. Oh, no."

"Oh, yes," he said. "So I proposed that the four of us meet for lunch. To plan our attack, you might say."

"Who's the fourth?"

"That's right – you were too drunk to hear about my meeting last evening." Janis *pshawed* but he ignored her, preferring to brief her on his session with Antoine and Simone.

"And since you were so convinced I was drunk that you never even asked me what I'd learned about Tandy ..." she said.

"There's more?" he asked.

"There's so much more." She filled him in on what she'd learned about her break with Carruthers, her Mexican misadventures, and how she lured Antoine in. "So this Simone," she said. "She's talented, isn't she?"

"I believe so, but I don't have any proof. I'm hoping the two of us can get her to reveal it before we meet with Tandy."

Janis heard the tiniest bit of hesitation in his voice. "She still scares you."

"She scares the hell out of me," he replied. "And it's unnerving to be pushing sixty and still feel this way."

"Not at all," she said. "We know a whole lot more about trauma now than we did forty years ago. That woman did a number on both of us."

"She scares you, too, doesn't she?"

"She never scared me," Janis scoffed. "I just want to punch her lights out. Where are we having lunch?"

"I thought I'd let you pick. They're staying at La Fonda."

Janis whistled low. "Nice place."

"I believe Simone picked it out."

"And put it on Tandy's tab, no doubt. I like her already." Janis grinned. "The hotel has an excellent restaurant. I'll call and get us a table for four. Noon okay?"

"I told Antoine 12:30, if that works for you."

"Why, Janusz Marek," she said with a pleased smile. "That's the first time I've ever heard you call that young man by his first name."

"I think we can help him, Janis," he said.

"I know we can. See you in a few hours."

Antoine was in the restaurant's lobby five minutes early. He paced restlessly, attracting stares from the maitre d' and other guests, but he didn't care. His whole world was falling down around his ears and he had no way to stop it.

He had dressed with more than his usual care: an actual suit, with matching blazer and slacks; an Oxford-cloth shirt with a button-down collar; and a sober tie. He had even had the concierge arrange to have his shoes polished. He had made an attempt to tame his dreads by pulling some of them into a ponytail, but all he had to hold them back was a rubber band and it kind of clashed with the rest of his outfit. So he gave up. His usual short, spiky 'do would have to serve.

Mr. Marek was bringing someone who he was sure Antoine would want to meet. But he didn't think he was ready right now to meet anyone new – this day was going to be stressful enough. He barely knew Mr. Marek, after all, and wasn't sure he was entirely trustworthy. Talented, yes, but the two didn't necessarily go hand in hand.

"Relax," Simone said from behind him. He turned and – he couldn't help it – he smiled broadly at her. She really was a good-looking woman. Today's hairstyle featured cornrows with a sleek blue-black bun attached at the crown of her head. It was both professional and regal, and once again he was torn between seeing her as a goddess or a queen. Her outfit was as sober as his, though – a navy blue blazer over a matching pencil skirt, with a gauzy scarf artfully arranged around her neck and secured with a pin. Her killer stilettos, together with the bun, gave her a couple of inches on him, but he didn't care. She was beautiful and she was his date.

"Hello, beautiful," he blurted.

"Hello, handsome," she returned with a pleased smile. "Now take your hands out of your pockets and roll your shoulders. Let go of some of that tension."

"Yes, ma'am," he said, doing as he was told.

"That's better," she said. Slipping her hand around his elbow, she urged him into a walk that was less pacing and more of a promenade.

They had made a couple of turns when Antoine tensed. "There he is," he said.

Simone smiled and waved like an excited kid, and Mr. Marek waved back. He was wearing what Antoine supposed was his usual work attire: a sports shirt and khakis, with brown loafers. He had thrown a blue blazer over the ensemble, but he could tell the man wasn't comfortable in it.

Antoine surveyed the woman with him. Like Simone, she wore a bun on top of her head, but hers was gray and not nearly as sleek. Her clothing was matronly: purple slacks and a flowered top, with a gray cardigan over it, and sensible shoes on her feet. Cats'-eye glasses completed the look. She looked like a teacher, or maybe a librarian. She was short – much shorter than Mr. Marek, who towered over Antoine – but for all that they looked like they ought to be mismatched, he got the sense that they were actually a set, that one would be incomplete without the other.

Names were exchanged and hands shaken all around. When Antoine greeted Mrs. Fowler, she held his hand in both of hers and looked at him with such kindness and understanding that he was tempted to fling himself into her arms. He contented himself with a grateful squeeze of her fingers. He still felt cautious around Mr. Marek, but Mrs. Fowler was his new favorite person in the world.

"Whose name is the reservation under?" Antoine asked.

"Mine," said Mrs. Fowler, and bustled up to the maitre d'.

"What a wonderful person," Simone said, watching her. "How long have you known her, Mr. Marek?"

"All my life," he said. His eyes never left her.

"Does she know Dr. Tandy as well?" Antoine asked.

That brought Mr. Marek's attention his way. "Let's get seated and order our food," he said. "Then we'll share our story with you."

"This way, everyone," Mrs. Fowler called. Mr. Marek went first, then Simone, and Antoine brought up the rear. That the position allowed him a view of her excellent ass was a pleasant coincidence.

"All right," said Janis as the waiter whisked their menus away and retreated. "I'll start, as I've known Tandy the longest."

"You mean Dr. Tandy," Antoine said.

She leveled a look at him. "I've known her for nearly sixty years," she said. "I'll call her whatever I like."

Antoine straightened. "Okay, then. Go ahead with your story."

"Thank you." She turned her gaze to Simone. "I was about two years old when my mother and grandmother dropped me off at the

Institute. My mother was a prostitute and a drug addict. She couldn't provide a stable home life for me, and she wouldn't give custody of me to my grandmother because her husband – my mother's stepfather – had sexually abused her for years when she was younger."

"I'm so sorry," Simone murmured.

"Which I knew about," Janis went on, "because I Saw it in my mother's memories. That's my talent," she told Antoine. "I read the past. And my mother believed her stepfather was my father. My grandmother refused to believe any of it had happened. So my mother turned me over to the Institute. She signed away her parental rights to Tandy the same day she met her.

"I was alone there – the only student at the Institute – for many years. Until the day Jan arrived." She turned to him and took a sip of water.

He picked up the cue admirably. "My talent is Seeing the future," he said. "My parents were at their wit's end with me – I was their only child and I wanted to be perfect for them, so I strove to get all the answers right." He chuckled. "But the way I got them was to look into the future and See the teacher's answer key. I could tell you the right answer but I couldn't work out the problem on my own, and I couldn't figure out why that wasn't enough for anybody. It ought to be, don't you think?"

The young people laughed politely. Janis squeezed his hand. He glanced at her and smiled, then resumed his tale. "So then there were two of us at the Institute. Antoine, that suite you're using as your office – is your office off the lounge and to the right?"

He sat back in surprise. "You mean the reception area? That big open room?"

"Right." Jan commandeered Janis's silverware and water glass to make a quick floor plan. "The front door is here. What you're calling the reception area was our lounge – our living room, in other words. Here's the kitchen."

"The pantry," Simone said.

"Okay. And the room off this hallway is your office, correct?"

"Correct." Antoine nodded.

"I thought so. That was my bedroom."

His face lit up. "No wonder you were so intent on the wall behind me!"

Jan nodded, grinning. "I can tell you the circumstances surrounding every nick in that bookcase."

"Where was your room, Mrs. Fowler?" Simone asked.

Janis grabbed one of Jan's forks to mark its place. "What are you using that room for now?" she asked.

"Storage," Simone said. "Printer supplies and things. I also use the bathroom in there."

"It's nice," Janis said. "I always thought so."

"It is," Simone agreed.

"So anyway," said Jan, disassembling the floor plan, "things went along pretty well for oh, four or five years. We had tutors for our classwork, and on certain afternoons Tandy had us try to stretch our talents. To make them more reliable, she said."

"But it was really so she could collect more information on the people she wanted us to See," Janis said. "And then she got *really* squirrelly."

"How so?" Antoine asked.

"Well," Janis said. "This isn't the sort of thing one usually discusses in mixed company. But once I started getting my periods, she began bringing in a doctor every few months to give me a gynecological exam."

"Why?" Simone asked.

"She wanted to know if my hymen was intact," Janis said bluntly. "She wanted to know if we were having sex."

"Why?" That was Antoine.

Jan took up the tale. "Her whole idea was to mate us. Like lab animals. She intended for us to produce an army of talented children who would be in thrall to her for as long as she wanted."

Antoine shook his head. "That's not how it works, though. That's not how genetics works for any trait."

"What was she going to do with the kids who weren't talented?" Simone asked.

The question hung heavily in the air. "We never asked," Janis said. After another moment, she went on. "When it became apparent to Tandy that we weren't going to make any babies for her, she sent me to have my tubes tied."

Simone gasped. "How could she get away with it?"

"She was my legal guardian. She claimed I was incapable of taking care of children because my talent made me unstable." Janis tried for a matter-of-fact tone, but didn't fully succeed.

"How awful for you," Simone said.

"Thank you," she said. "But what she did to Jan was just as bad. She undermined his belief in himself. She called him stupid and told him his talent was worthless."

"And at the same time," Jan said, "she was trying to get me to have sex with her." He looked at Antoine. "Does any of this sound familiar to you?"

"Yeah, it does," Antoine murmured. "It does. So what happened?"

"She raped me," Jan said. That brought another gasp from Simone. "By this time, Janis and I were nearly eighteen, and I couldn't see any way that we could get out. So I tried to kill myself."

"Oh, my God," Simone said.

"Lucky for us," Janis continued, "Ray Carruthers' nephew took the call about Jan's suicide attempt. He met me at the hospital – I'd ridden with Jan in the ambulance – and he rescued us. Within forty-eight hours, we had our own apartment and money for college, all courtesy of the Institute."

"Well, courtesy of Carruthers," Jan said.

"Regardless. Jake saved us."

"And you want to pay it forward," Simone said. She traded a look with Antoine.

"I guess you could call it that," Janis said. "So now you've heard our stories. Let's hear yours."

At that moment, the food arrived. It was another few minutes before the conversation resumed.

Antoine went first. "Well, mine is so similar to Mr. Marek's that there's not much more to tell. My talent is creating such convincing scenarios in people's minds that they believe they're true."

"I can vouch for that," Jan said. "You pulled me in twice."

"Ah, but the second time it didn't work as well. You knew it was coming," Antoine said. "In any case, by the time I was ten, I'd driven my parents so crazy that they were happy to sign whatever papers Dr. Tandy put in front of them. I've been living at FAE since then. And she has treated me much as she treated you, Mr. Marek."

"Please call me Jan," he said.

"And I'm Janis," she put in.

Antoine nodded. "All right. Thank you. So anyway, Dr. Tandy …"

Simone interrupted him. "She says the most awful things to him. She calls him names all the time. On the one hand, she gave him this fancy title – Vice President of Global Operations – but there isn't any global operation and she still makes all the decisions."

"She was livid when she found out we'd come here without consulting her first," Antoine said.

"And she's sleeping with you," Jan said.

"Yeah," Antoine admitted, looking down at his plate. "It … yeah."

"Antoine, can I tell you something I've Seen in your future?" Jan asked.

His head came up. "Am I going to like it?"

"Nope."

He put his fork down and leaned his forearms on the table on either side of his plate. "All right. Go ahead."

208

Jan's gaze met his. "She's using you. She wants access to NASA's communication systems so you can find more talent for her. She's still trying to build an army of talented people to control. And once you get her those talents, she'll wash her hands of you."

He nodded. "That's about what I'd figured out. But how do I get out? You guys had help. I don't have anyone."

"I think you do," Janis said, and turned to Simone. "Tell us, dear. What's your talent?"

Simone locked gazes with her. "How did you know?"

"That was me," Jan said.

"Wait. You …?" Antoine said, pointing at Simone.

Jan went on, "When I Saw Antoine's future, I noticed something I'd never seen before – a concurrent timeline running alongside his, trying to intersect with his. That was you, wasn't it?"

She nodded. "It was. My talent" – she took a breath and started over – "my talent is keeping people safe. I only wish it had worked for my brother. But my talent was no match for Dr. Tandy."

As Janis stared at her, the young woman's history rolled out before her eyes. "Oh, you poor dear," she said. "I am so very sorry."

"What happened?" Jan asked.

"Remember I told you about Tandy's activities in Central America? The child prostitution ring she ran?"

Antoine stared at Simone. "My God. You never told me."

"No, I didn't," she said. "I thought this job would give me the opportunity for vengeance. But I'm not cut out for vengeance." She looked at all of them. "And she is so much worse than I ever dreamed she was."

"Vengeance only begets vengeance," Jan said. "Rather think of it in terms of justice being served."

"We have always believed that choices have consequences," Janis said. "It's time Tandy faced the consequences of all the vile choices she has made."

Jan nodded. "Agreed. When and where are you meeting her?"

"Right here." He checked the time on his phone. "In about an hour."

"Then we have time for dessert," Jan said. "I believe I'll have something alcoholic."

Antoine felt as though he were in his element. He was really good at messing with people's heads. *Really* good at it. Especially when the target deserved what they had coming.

So he was perfectly relaxed as he sat in the hotel's reception area, waiting for Denise to show up. She did, finally, and she was clearly not in a good mood.

As she entered, he stood and waved her over. "Denise!" he called genially. "So good to see you again. How was your flight?"

"Cramped," she complained. "The flight was nearly sold out. I got stuck in a middle seat."

"That sounds awful," he said. "And how was the drive? Was the traffic okay? Is your rental car acceptable?"

"Don't try your obsequious act with me," she said tartly. "You have screwed up this project from the start. I don't know what possessed me to promote you to Vice President of Global Operations in the first place. I ought to fire you right now. But here I am instead, pulling your bacon out of the fire again."

"Would you like to check in?" Antoine asked, the friendly smile never leaving his face.

"*No*, I would not like to check in. I would like to get this business over with so I can go home." She looked around. "I thought I told you to have that man meet us here."

"Mr. Marek?" Antoine said. "Oh, he's here."

"Well, where is he?" she demanded.

"Right here, Denise," said Jan, stepping around a corner. "And I've brought along another old friend."

Janis stepped out to stand next to him. "Hello, Denise. Long time no see." She squinted through her glasses. "I must say, your plastic surgeon did a wonderful job. You can hardly see any scarring."

"Only the best for the special friend of El Serpiente," said Simone, stepping out of an adjacent alcove.

"What in the …? Simone, is that you? What do you know about El Serpiente?" Tandy scoffed. She looked around at the four of them. "What is the meaning of this?"

Simone strode to Tandy's side and handed her a photo. "Does this little boy look familiar?" she challenged.

Tandy hardly glanced at the photo. "No," she said, tossing it on the cocktail table in front of her.

"He should," Simone said. "His name was Pedro Moreno and he was my brother. You sold him to a man who *used* him." Her breath came out in little sobs. "And then *killed* him. My baby brother was only nine years old, Dr. Tandy."

"About the same age as I was when I came to the Institute," Jan said.

"Only a year younger than I was when I came to FAE," Antoine said.

"You're a murderer, Dr. Tandy," Simone said, her voice rising. "You're an abuser of children, a grifter, and a thief. And the Mexican police are still looking for you."

"So are the New Mexico State Police," said Jan, "for scamming Jemez Aerospace. And the FBI for your attempt to scam NASA."

While the others spoke, Antoine worked his magic, as he liked to think of it. He found the fear in Denise's mind and built on it: her run for the Mexican border just before the Instutute's investors descended to pick over the carcass; her panic when she heard that the Mexican cops had arrested El Serpiente, and her headlong flight back to the States before they could catch her; the day Antoine had, at her direction, sweet-talked the honchos at Jemez into signing the contract with FAE.

211

Now he led her thoughts down the path he wanted them to follow. She had spent so much time trying to make her life easier, but it just kept getting more complicated! She couldn't spend the rest of her life in prison. She just couldn't!

"No!" she cried out. "I paid my debt to society!"

"When?" Janis said, laughing at her. "I've Seen your past, Denise."

"How?" Denise said in horror, as Antoine again played on her fears. "You couldn't have! I buried those memories as soon as I knew you could See them!"

"It doesn't matter how," Janis went on relentlessly. She stepped toward her. "I've Seen how many times you've run from justice. I've Seen how you left others holding the bag time and time again. Well, no more! No more running. Choices have consequences, Denise Tandy, and you are about to experience the consequences of *yours*!"

Antoine's magic surrounded Denise with a cordon of shadowy authorities.

With a scream, she bolted from her chair and ran for the door. Antoine followed her, the better to keep the illusion alive, and the others followed on his heels.

Out the door and across the historic plaza Denise ran – right into a couple of Santa Fe city police officers. When one of them grabbed her to try to calm her down, she struck him. That got her handcuffed and shoved into a squad car. The police then got into the car and drove away.

Antoine, Simone, Janis, and Jan stood stock-still on the sidewalk for a few moments. Then Janis said, "I need to sit down," and headed back into the hotel. The others trailed after her.

Sinking into the chair Denise had recently vacated, Janis sighed in relief. "That's better. Too much excitement for one day." She looked up at Antoine, Simone, and Jan. "So. What do you think will happen to her?"

"If I had to guess," Antoine said, "she's probably babbling about her innocence to the cops right now. Once they piece together the details, I'm sure they'll find something to jail her for."

"Resisting arrest, for starters," Jan said. He clapped Antoine on the shoulder. "Congratulations, Champ. You're free."

Chapter 31 — A few months later

Janis looked up from her tablet as Jan came down the hallway, yawning and scratching his head. "Good morning, lazybones," she said with a smile. "Nice bedhead you've got there."

He belted his robe a little more tightly around his waist before leaning down to give her a kiss. "Thanks. Took me all night to cultivate it." He shuffled into the kitchen. "What's for breakfast?"

"I was thinking French toast," she said. "Coffee's fresh."

"Already on it," he said, pouring himself a cup. Then he settled next to her on her couch. "Anything new and interesting in the world?"

"Well," she said, "you already knew about Tandy's trial." The police had indeed charged her with resisting arrest. And when they ran her fingerprints, they discovered Simone hadn't been lying — the Mexican authorities really *were* looking for her in connection with her role in El Serpiente's drug cartel. She had an extradition hearing scheduled in Albuquerque within the next few weeks.

"Right," he said. "Couldn't happen to a nicer psychopath."

"You always say that," she said, slapping his arm.

"Hey! You could have spilled my coffee," he complained.

"Don't be such a goofball, then. Oh — Simone emailed me."

He sipped from his mug and set it down on the coffee table. "Good news, I hope."

"It is. Antoine's got a new job. Selling real estate."

Jan smiled. "I could not have picked a better career for him. Which reminds me."

Janis rolled her eyes. "Not this again."

"But we should consolidate, sweetheart," he said. "And my house is bigger. Why don't you want to give this place up?"

"I like having my own space," she said. "Besides, the commute would be terrible. Forty-five minutes one way? No, thank you."

He sighed. "Stubborn."

"Yes, I am. And I come by it honestly." She kissed his scratchy cheek. "Hey." He turned to her and their lips met. "I do love you. And I do want to live with you. I just need more time, okay?"

"All right," he said, wrapping an arm around her shoulders. "But I'm going to keep asking, you know."

"If you didn't, I'd be looking for the pod in the basement," she said, snuggling into his chest.

"Pod in the …?" He exploded in laughter. "What on earth are you talking about?"

She sat up and stared at him. "You've never seen *Invasion of the Body Snatchers?*"

"No," he said.

"Then I know what *we're* doing today," she said, reaching for the remote. "Now, which version should we watch first – the 1956 original, or the 1978 remake?"

"Oh, we should go chronologically, by all means," he said.

"I'm glad we agree."

He swiped the remote. "But first, breakfast."

"That's what I love about you, Jan," she said. "You're so practical."

Author's Note

You know how everything changed at the start of the pandemic? How some of us were able to work from home and others were stuck out on the front lines, exposing themselves to terrible unknowns in order to make a living? And remember how some influencers tried to encourage those of us sheltering at home to use our time constructively – to learn a new language or tackle that novel we'd always wanted to write? That sort of thing?

And then remember how we were so overwhelmed by dealing with everything associated with the pandemic – hunting for hand sanitizer and toilet paper, finding or sewing masks, trying to make a living while having the kids underfoot all day – that almost none of our grand, creative, constructive plans came to pass?

I sure do. This novel is the first full-length work of fiction I've written since the pandemic began. I got *Beach Magic* out the door when the lockdown was new, and then gave Camp NaNo over to journaling. Then over the summer, I retired from the day job and moved from northern Virginia to New Mexico. All that *and* the pandemic, too! Getting back into writing mode for NaNoWriMo in November was almost painful; editing what I'd written was even harder to contemplate.

But I think this book is better for its extra-long ripening. I needed the time away to realize that it's not just a love story between two geezers, but a story about patience – and balance, and justice.

Thanks again to Susan Strayer for her usual diligent editing. This book would be much more of a mishmash without her help. And thanks to my Facebook friends, upon whom I inflicted draft book covers and possible titles before I hit on the winners.

Speaking of justice, my Facebook author page is no more. Over the years, hackers had made several attempts to get control of it, but in November they succeeded. I was able to regain control of the page eventually, but then decided it wasn't worth the hassle to keep it. So the Woo-Woo Team group is now your best bet for reaching me there.

Nobody can hack my newsletter (that I'm aware of), so feel free to sign up at http://eepurl.com/xxw9d; that's the most reliable way for you to know when I have a new book coming out.

And of course, as always, you can always leave a review wherever you bought this book. Reviews let other readers know what you thought of a book, and I'm grateful to everyone who posts one. Thank you!

Lynne Cantwell
May 2021

About the Author

Lynne Cantwell writes mostly urban fantasy and paranormal romance, with a dash of magic realism when she's feeling more serious. She is also a contributing author for Indies Unlimited. In a previous life, she was a broadcast journalist who worked at Mutual/NBC Radio News, CNN, and a bunch of other places you have probably never heard of. She has a master's degree in fiction writing from Johns Hopkins University. She lives in New Mexico.

Discover other novels by Lynne Cantwell:

The Elemental Keys
River Magic (original title: Rivers Run)
Bog Magic (original title: Treacherous Ground)
Gecko Magic (original title: Molten Trail)
Beach Magic

The Pipe Woman Chronicles Universe
Seized: Book One of the Pipe Woman Chronicles
Fissured: Book Two of the Pipe Woman Chronicles
Tapped: Book Three of the Pipe Woman Chronicles
Gravid: Book Four of the Pipe Woman Chronicles
Annealed: Book Five of the Pipe Woman Chronicles
The Pipe Woman Chronicles Omnibus

Where Were You When: A Land, Sea, Sky Anthology
Crosswind: Land, Sea, Sky Book 1
Undertow: Land, Sea, Sky Book 2
Scorched Earth: Land, Sea, Sky Book 3
The Land Sea Sky Trilogy

Dragon's Web: Book One of the Pipe Woman's Legacy
Firebird's Snare: Book Two of the Pipe Woman's Legacy
Spider's Lifeline: Book Three of the Pipe Woman's Legacy
Turtle's Weir: Book Four of the Pipe Woman's Legacy

A Billion Gods and Goddesses: The Mythology Behind *The Pipe Woman Chronicles*

The Transcendence Trilogy
Maggie in the Dark: Transcendence Book 1
Maggie on the Cusp: Transcendence Book 2
Maggie at Moonrise: Transcendence Book 3

Stand-Alone Novels
SwanSong
Seasons of the Fool
The Payoff

Short Story Collections
Back Home Again: The Five59 Stories, plus a few

Find Lynne on Teh Intarwebz:

Facebook: http://www.facebook.com/groups/WooWooTeam
Twitter: http://twitter.com/lynnecantwell
Goodreads:
http://www.goodreads.com/author/show/696603.Lynne_Cantwell
Pinterest: http://pinterest.com/lynnecantwell
Ravelry: https://www.ravelry.com/people/lynnecm
Blog: http://www.hearth-myth.com